RUSE™

ENTER THE DETECTIVE

RUSE™
ENTER THE DETECTIVE

Mark **WAID**
W R I T E R

Butch **GUICE**
P E N C I L E R

Mike **PERKINS**
I N K E R

Laura **MARTIN**
C O L O R I S T

CHAPTER 6

Jeff **JOHNSON** · PENCILER
Paul **NEARY** · INKER
Jason **LAMBERT** · COLORIST

Dave **LANPHEAR** · LETTERER

CrossGeneration Comics   **Oldsmar, Florida**

ENTER THE DETECTIVE

features Chapters One through Six
from the ongoing series RUSE.

BARONESS BEGUILING

❧ OUR PLAYERS ❧

SIMON ARCHARD
THE CITY'S FAVORITE SON,
HIS MIND IS RAZOR-SHARP

EMMA BISHOP
A FETCHING BEAUTY,
HER SPIRIT CRAVES ADVENTURE

MIRANDA CROSS
A MYSTERIOUS VISITOR,
SOMETHING BUBBLES BENEATH HER SURFACE

SHE VISITS OUR SHORES

PARTINGTON societal circles are awhirl with the arrival of one Miranda Cross, Baroness of the Eastern land of Kharibast. According to her local hosts, Lord and Lady Wainscott of the Blumjuine district, Baroness Cross plans to set up permanent residence in our fair city and has already begun shipping crates of exotic finery and *objets d'art* to the site of her new mansion, all but completed as of this writing.

The Baroness, who came to international fame after parlaying her late husband's ailing estate into a veritable kingdom of wealth and political power, has spent the last eighteen months touring the world. She is accompanied in her travels by a small entourage of servants uncommon, few of whom are versed in the King's language and thus are best approached with patience and caution.

WAINSCOTTS TO INTRODUC

Lord and Lady Wainscott have announced a grand ball to be held at their manor at week's end, at which time Baroness Cross will be formally introduced to Partington's favored citizens and its brokers of power.

BANKER MURDERED

EARS SLICED, STOLEN!

PARTINGTON police yesterday found the body of banker Charles X. Victor, a victim of foul play. While no suspects have yet been detained, Hughes' partner, Edgar Murchand, has himself posted a sizeable reward for any information leading to the arrest and prosecution of the villainous soul or soul responsible.

Most curious was the dissected stat of Victor's corpse, leaving city wag to dub this the "Victorian Ear Mystery." No photoengravings have bee released **•••PLEASE CONTINUE INSID**

1.1

PLEASE, MR. MURCHAND. THE BELLOWS *ALONE*...! ⇥SIGH⇤

SIMON--?

YES, EMMA. "YOUR REPUTATION *PRECEDES* YOU, SIMON." "YOU'VE DONE IT *AGAIN*, MILORD." "*KUDOS*."

IF YOU'RE LOOKING FOR A *RESPONSE* THIS TIME, TRY *THIS* ONE:

"*TAXI!*"

SIMON!

Oh, OF *COURSE*.

THE INEVITABLE "*ESCAPE*." AREN'T THERE ANY *ORIGINAL* CRIMINALS LEFT IN THIS WORLD?

STAY BACK OR THE GIRL *DIES!*

I WILL NOT BE *JAILED!*

EEEEE!

SIMON, THE *GIRL!* SHE'S *TERRIFIED*, AND FOR *GOOD REASON!*

I *BEG* YOU, CHOOSE YOUR WORDS *CAREFULLY!*

DON'T BE A *FOOL*, MURCHAND. *SURRENDER* IS YOUR ONLY *OPTION*. WHERE IS THERE TO *RUN?* CONSIDER THE *ASPHALTUM* BENEATH YOUR FEET.

I *MEAN* IT! STAY *BACK* OR--

ASPHALTUM?

A PARTICULARLY *INFERIOR* GRADE IN THIS NEIGHBORHOOD, ALREADY SUBJECTED TO DEGRADATION FROM SUN EXPOSURE, ONLY *WEAKENED* BY THE RAIN.

SIMON--!

IT'S WHAT SECURES THE *BARRIER* YOU'VE PRESSED AGAINST.

I PUT YOUR WEIGHT AT 230 POUNDS, HERS AT 106.

AND A *HALF*.

THE ASPHALTUM SUPPORTS PERHAPS 275.

AT BEST.

AAAAH!

AAAH--

--AAAH--

--AAAH--

EEEEEEEEEE! EE!

1.2

1.3

1.4

1.5

1.9

MY NAME IS **EMMA BISHOP.** SOME CALL ME THE PARTNER OF **SIMON ARCHARD,** THE WORLD'S GREATEST DETECTIVE.

OTHERS REFER TO ME MERELY HIS **ASSISTANT.**

EVEN FOR ALL THE **KNOWLEDGE** IN SIMON'S **HEAD,** HE SIMPLY WON'T **BOTHER** TO LEARN **FOREIGN LANGUAGES.** HE ARGUES THAT THE ART OF **COMMUNICATION** IS ONE BEST MASTERED ON A SUBTLE, **NON-VERBAL** LEVEL.

I DISAGREE.

WELL, ONLY **ONE** OTHER, ACTUALLY.

THAT WOULD BE SIMON.

WHO'S DRAGGING ME OUT TO **WAINSCOTT MANOR** AND SOME **COMING OUT PARTY** FOR SOME **OVER-SEAS ROYALTY** OR SOME-SUCH FOL-DE-ROL... IN THE EVENT, I SUPPOSE, THAT MY **LINGUISTIC SKILLS** MIGHT BE OF SOME AID.

IT'S A QUARREL DIFFICULT TO **WIN** SEEING AS HOW, IN GENERAL, PEOPLE DON'T REALLY ENJOY **TALKING** TO HIM.

SIMON'S POSITION IN *SOCIETAL CIRCLES* HAS MORE TO DO WITH HIS *REPUTATION* THAN HIS... *CHARM.* I'M SURE HE THINKS HE'S BEING *HELPFUL,* BUT FOR ALL HIS *GIFTS...* WELL...

SIMON! HOW *WONDERFUL* TO SEE YOU AND *IRMA* AGAIN!

EMMA.

GILES, TAKE IRMA'S *WRAP* WITH SIMON'S COAT.

RIGHT *AWAY,* MADAM.

...*SMALL TALK* ISN'T REALLY *AMONG* THEM.

HOW MANY COATS *HAS* THAT SERVANT TAKEN TONIGHT, LADY WAINSCOTT?

POLICE COMMISSIONER *THORNTON* IS, AFTER ALL THESE YEARS, UNIQUELY *ACCUSTOMED TO* SIMON'S MANNER.

SIMON! ELLA!

EMMA.

JUST HEARD ABOUT THE *MURCHAND* ARREST.

DETECTIVE HABER TELLS ME HE WAS ABLE TO FULLY *EXPLAIN* THE MURDER THIS TIME *BEFORE* YOU FINGERED THE CULPRIT.

YOU'RE *SLIPPING.*

I'M GLAD TO SEE THE RISE IN *GROTTESCAPHOBIA* DIDN'T KEEP YOU *AWAY.*

FEAR OF *GARGOYLES?*

THEY *DO* TEND TO *FLIT* ABOUT LIKE *BATS,* COMMISSIONER, BUT...

ACTUALLY, THEY'VE *EATEN* THE *BATS.*

Oh.

HOW FARES THE DEPARTMENT THESE DAYS, THEOPOLOUS?

POORLY, I'M AFRAID. THIS *MORAL DECAY* I'VE BEEN ON ABOUT?

IT'S *VERY REAL,* SIMON. THE SIMPLE *GRIFT* OR *BAGSNATCH* IS QUICKLY BECOMING A THING OF THE *PAST.*

WHY... *ALL* OF THEM...? I SUPPOSE...? WHY?

BECAUSE ONE WONDERS HOW MANY VALUABLES HE'S *ALREADY* FILCHED FROM THEIR *POCKETS* AND PASSED THROUGH THE WINDOW TO HIS ASSOCIATE *OUTSIDE*.

SHALL WE?

LET'S.

TRUTH TO TELL, IT DOESN'T MATTER *WHOSE* KITCHEN SIMON *IS IN.*

HE'LL *ALWAYS* STIR THE POT.

WHY, JUST TODAY, MY MEN HAD TO DEAL WITH AN ATTEMPTED RITUAL *SUICIDE* DOWNTOWN...A *MAD DOG* TERRORIZING THE DOCKS...*AND* A GANG OF TEENAGERS--

--*TEENAGERS!*--

--WHO WERE FENCING STOLEN GOODS TO FUEL THEIR *MEDICINAL CACOETHES!*

ADDICTIONS? TO *WHAT?*

THERE'S AN *OPIATE* PROBLEM DAWNING IN THIS TOWN. A WAVE OF *INEXPENSIVE DRUGS* IS SWEEPING PARTINGTON, TEMPTING THE YOUNG AND OLD ALIKE WITH AN UPLIFTING *EUPHORIA...*

...THAT, I PRESUME, TOO *OFTEN* ENDS IN *MADNESS.*

QUITE RIGHT, SIMON, YOU'VE BEEN COMPLAINING FOR *SOME TIME* THAT OUR FAIR BURG NO LONGER PRESENTS YOU WITH MEANINGFUL *CHALLENGES.*

I'D *GLADLY* SUFFER YOUR *ENNUI* AS THE PRICE *PAID* IF THAT WERE *TRUE,* BUT IT MAY *NOT* BE ERE *LONG.* ONE *CANNOT HELP* BUT *WONDER:*

WHATEVER NEW EVIL WILL VISIT US *NEXT?*

IF I MAY...

1.13

1.14

PLEASE [AL]LOW MY [INT]RODUCTION, [M]R. ARCHARD. IT IS [IN]FREQUENT I [CR]OSS THE PATH [W]ITH ONE SO [C]ELEBRATED.

AND YET, YOU *KNOW* ME.

OF YOU.

EVEN IN *KHARIB*--?

A MAN OF *WONDER*... YES, HE IS. I'M--

...AND *SURPRISING HANDSOMENESS*.

OH, DEAR.

WELL... *ANTAEUS*, IS IT? *GREETINGS*-- OR SHOULD I SAY "MALEV *TOFIN*"?

"DIER *THON*"?

"PEÑAN-PENÁN"?

HELLO?

...AND, NATURALLY, [T]HE SKILL WITH WHICH [Y]OU UNRAVELED THE [F]ORSYTHE CONUNDRUM [...]MADE...*PAPERS*?...

PRESS. *YES*.

...IN *MY* HOMELAND.

I HAVE *CLIPPINGS* IF YOU'D CARE TO *READ* THEM SOME TIME. COME *BY* AND WE'LL --

-- MR. ARCHARD?

Oh. I HAVE... BROUGHT HIM *BOREDOM*?

HARDLY, BARONESS. HE FINDS *THAT* ON HIS *OWN*. IT'S NOTHING *PERSONAL*.

AND YOU MUST BE *EMMA*.

→SIGH← FOR THE *LAST TIME*, MY NAME IS-- oh. EMMA. YES, EMMA.

YOUR LOVER IS RATHER... *SINGLE-MINDED*, NO?

MADAM! HE IS *HARDLY* MY... MY... OUR RELATIONSHIP IS PURELY *PROFESSIONAL!*

Hmmm.

AND I PREFER TO THINK OF SIMON AS "*FOCUSED*."

AN *ATTRACTIVE QUALITY*...

...DEPENDING ON WHAT COMMANDS HIS *ATTENTION*.

OR WHO?

PERHAPS. GOOD *EVENING*, MISS BISHOP.

ARE YOU GONE?

THEN NOT YET, IT ISN'T.

1.15

WITH THE REWARD FROM THE **CARRINGTON AFFAIR**, SIMON REFURBISHED AN ABANDONED **CATHEDRAL** IN THE **NORTHSHIRE** PART OF TOWN AND MADE IT HIS **HOME** AND **HEADQUARTERS**. IT HOUSES SIMON'S **INVENTIONS**, HIS **LABORATORIES**, AND A LIBRARY **LEGENDARY** FOR ITS SIZE.

NEITHER **GATED** NOR **SECLUDED**, THE BUILDING IS **READILY ACCESSIBLE** TO **ALL**. NEVERTHELESS, WHILE OUR SERVICES SEEM OFTEN IN **DEMAND**, ONE DOESN'T SIMPLY WALK IN TO SIMON ARCHARD'S HOME AND ASK FOR **HELP**.

ADMITTANCE REQUIRES... QUITE *LITERALLY*...A "SCREENING PROCESS."

STAND HERE

STATE YOUR BUSINESS.

NAME'S McCORKINDALE. Y'WOU'NT *KNOW* ME...

...BUT'A COME T'SEE MR. ARCHARD.

1.17

THE POOR MAN **TREMBLED**, THOUGH WHETHER A RESULT OF **NERVES** OR A **BOTTLE**, I COULD NOT SAY. NOT THAT YOU COULD **CONDEMN** HIM FOR SIPPING **WHISKEY**.

NOT WITH THE **SORROW** IN THOSE **EYES**.

...AWARE 'TAINT TH' KINDA HIGH-FALUTIN' CASE WHAT YOU'RE **KNOWN** F'R, SIR...

...BUT TH' BOYS DOWN A' THE **DOCK** PUT SOME COIN T'GETHER TO **HIRE** YE IF IT'S A QUESTION O' **MONEY**.

MONEY IS **NEVER** THE QUESTION. TELL ME ABOUT THE **VICTIM**.

O'SHAUGHNESSY IS-- --WAS--HIS NAME. A **LEGENDARY** CAP'N IN HIS DAY HE WAS--B'LOVED BY **ALL** TH' DOCKWORKERS 'N' FISHERMEN, SIR. SWEARIN' NE'ER T'BREATHE NOTHIN' BUT **SALT** AIR, HE KEPT A RUM LI'L **SHACK** RIGHT THERE ON TH' **PIER**, AN' WE ALL **TENDED** T'HIM.

S'WHY WHA' **HAPPEN** MADE **NO** SENSE A'TALL.

RUN THROUGH A **DOZEN** TIMES 'RE MORE, HE WAS... KNIFED 'N' GORED...LEFT FLOATIN' UNDER THE **PIER**...BUT **WHY?** T'WEREN'T NO **ROBBERY**... O'SHAUGHNESSY NE'ER HAD TWO **PENNIES** T'JINGLE.

I IMAGINE **NOT**.

I CAN'T **HELP** YOU, McCORKINDALE. THIS IS A ROUTINE **POLICE** MATTER WIT NOT ENOUGH **CLUE** AND TOO MANY **SUSPECTS**.

THE DOCKS ARE **FULL** OF UNSAVORY CHARACTERS AND GOINGS-ON. DOUBTLES THE OLD MAN SAW O OVERHEARD SOMETHIN THAT HE WASN'T **SUPPOSED** TO AND WAS **SILENCED**.

THAT'S THE ONLY **EXPLANATIO**

...

REALLY.

When forger **EUGENE FEINSILBER** was kidnapped from a **LOCKED PRISON CELL**, SIMON **YAWNED** AND SOLVED THE CASE WHILE COMPLETING A **CROSSWORD PUZZLE**.

WHEN THE DUCHESS OF LARTUUM'S ENTIRE **SUMMER HOME** WAS STOLEN RIGHT DOWN TO THE **STABLES**, HE PLACED A **TELEPHONE CALL** DURING HIS **MANICURE** AND MADE HEADLINES BEFORE **DINNER**.

THIS TIME, HE'S ACTUALLY ON HIS **FEET**. IS THERE SOMETHING TO THIS CASE THAT STRIKES A **CHORD** WITHIN HIM? DOES IT **MATTER**?

ALL I'M **SURE** OF IS THAT THERE'S A GLINT IN SIMON'S EYES I'VE NOT **SEEN** BEFORE.

I DON'T THINK SO, SIR. SEE, THERE'S SOMETHIN' I HA'N'T MENTIONED YET. HE COULDN'TA HEARD **NOTHIN'** WHAT WOULD HAVE CAUSED ANYONE NO **TROUBLE**, 'CAUSIN' O'SHAUGHNESSY...

...HE WAS **BLIND 'N'** ALL BUT **DEAF**.

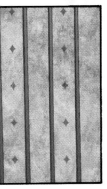

AS THE AFTERNOON PROGRESSES, WE SORT THROUGH THE VICTIM O'SHAUGHNESSY'S PERSONAL EFFECTS... WE SPEAK TO THOSE WHO KNEW HIM...WE COMB HIS LAST-KNOWN WHEREABOUTS...ALL OF WHICH LEADS US TO...

...NOTHING.

THE FACT THAT SOMEONE'S NOT ALREADY IN *JAIL* DOESN'T SPEAK WELL OF OUR *TRADITIONAL* METHODS, SIMON.

YOU *CLAIM* ALL SOLUTIONS EMERGE FROM *LOGIC* AND *EVIDENCE*... BUT EVEN YOU CAN SEE HOW *TEDIOUS* INTELLECTUAL *PUZZLES* EVENTUALLY BECOME.

GIVEN *THAT*, I DON'T *ACCEPT* THAT THERE'S NOT MORE *DRIVING* YOU THAN *MORBID CURIOSITY*. WE WOULDN'T DO WHAT WE *DO* IF YOU HADN'T, AT SOME POINT, *FELT* A NEED TO *HELP* PEOPLE. HADN'T REALIZED THERE'S AN ENTIRE *WORLD* BEYOND THE TIP OF YOUR *NOSE*.

WHATEVER CAUSED YOU TO *FORGET*... OR *IGNORE*... THAT?

STRANGE.

CRATES ON A *LOADING DOCK?*

UNDER A *NEWLY SHREDDED TARPAULIN*, CONTAINED BY *FRESHLY FRAYED ROPES*.

YOU'RE INVADING A *CRIME SCENE.*

I'M *SITTING* WHERE *O'SHAUGHNESSY* SAT EACH DAY, SIMON. I'M TRYING TO SEE THE WORLD THROUGH THE *VICTIM'S* EYES-- SO TO *SPEAK*--

--IMAGINING A LIFE WHERE THE COMPANIONSHIP OF A *DOG* HAS TO COMPENSATE FOR *SENSES* THAT HAVE *ATROPHIED.*

IT'S MY METHOD OF ACQUIRING SOME BETTER *SENSE* OF IT ALL. PONDERING THE *WHY* OF IT.

...HERE *IS* A HEART INSIDE *YOUR* CHEST, SIMON...

...AND I *WILL REINTRODUCE* THE TWO OF YOU IF IT'S THE LAST THING I...

...oh, BLOODY *HELL.*

SIMON...?

OH!

A NGUAGE YOU ECOGNIZE?

EMMA?

GAARN! GAARN FAUTO *JUNGAI!*

HE WANTS US TO *LEAVE. NOW.*

JUNGAI *TATEEN!*

ASK IF WE CAN EXAMINE WHAT'S UNDER THE *TARPAULIN.*

I DON'T THINK I *HAVE* TO. *JUNGAI!*

SUSPICIOUS.

QUITE. CAN YOU *PRESS* THE POINT WITHOUT RISKING GRAVE BODILY *HARM?*

I *DOUBT* IT.

THEN WE *LEAVE.*

RATHER *ELEGANT* OF YOU.

ON THE *CONTRARY...*

1.21

JUNGAI FALA ROTHAN! TAY ROTHANNNN!

START WALKING.

⇒AHUH⇐ AHUH

...A LITTLE... WINDED...

INTO THE ALLEY. HURRY.

THESE AREN'T... RUNNING SHOES, SIMON...

...ARE THEY STILL ⇒AHUH⇐ BEHIND US?

GOODNESS! WE... ⇒AHUH⇐ ...WE CERTAINLY SHOWED THEM, DIDN'T WE!

YOU STAND IN THE WAY OF THE GREAT SIMON ARCHARD...

...AND HE'LL SPILL YOUR FISH! AH HAHA HA HA...!

A RHAPASTANIAN EPITHET! DEAR GOD, SIMON --

-- THERE'S YOUR MURDERER! SOMEHOW, O'SHAUGHNESSY RAN AFOUL OF THE CULT OF PHARSA!

SINISTER.

AND UNSTOPPABLE! SIMON, THIS GOES DEEPER THAN WE EVER COULD HAVE --

NO.

NNGHH!

"SINISTER" -- AS IN LEFT.

THE PHARSANS ALWAYS --

⇒HNNFF!⇐

-- ALWAYS HOLD THEIR SCYTHES IN THEIR LEFT "UNCLEAN" HAND --

-- NEVER THEIR RIGHT!

THIS IMPOSTOR HAS BEEN SENT TO RATHER CLUMSILY LEAD US DOWN A FALSE TRAIL, EMMA!

1.23

AIEEEE!

FWUMPH

WHAT?

SPEND THE NEXT *HOUR* GATHERING *POLICEMEN* AT SIMON'S *BEHEST* WHILE HE DASHES AROUND THE *WATER-FRONT* LOOKING FOR ONE OFFICER IN *PARTICULAR...* THOUGH *WHY* AND TO WHAT *END...?*

VERIFY IT FOR ME, OFFICER. HE WAS ROUGHLY 120 POUNDS... WHITE HAIR... A *DANE?*

YES, SIR. THAT'S THE *ONE.*

YOU'LL *RECALL* THE COMMISSIONER MENTIONING A *MAD HOUND* THAT WAS PUT *DOWN* YESTERDAY-- BY *THIS* POLICEMAN.

THE UNFORTUNATE BEAST WAS NO *MERE* VICTIM OF *DISEASE,* HOWEVER.

HE WAS DRIVEN *WILD* BY THE *SCENT* OF THOSE *FISH.*

FISH? BUT HOW--?

OUR *SEAFARING FRIENDS* ARE LESS *FISHERMEN...*

...THAN *SMUGGLERS.*

OFFICERS, IF YOU'LL *EXAMINE* THEIR *CARGO*--

--YOU'LL FIND NUMEROUS *PHIALS* MADE OF BADLY DISCOLORED *METAL* AND CONTAINING--

...KILLING THE OLD MAN FOR WHAT THEY *FEARED* HE'D SEEN BEFORE EVEN *REALIZING...* IF THEY *EVER DID...* THAT HE WAS *SIGHTLESS* AND OF *NO THREAT.*

THE *DOG, MADDENED* BY THE *DRUGS,* GOT *AWAY* ONLY TO BE MISTAKEN AS *RABID* AND *SHOT.*

OFFICER, IF YOU CAN... *EXTRACT* FROM THESE RAKEHELLS THE NAME AND WHEREABOUTS OF THEIR *CAPTAIN,* WE'LL LEAVE THE *PROSECUTION* TO *YOU.*

--NARCOTICS.

A CLEVER BUT *RISKY* WAY TO IMPORT THEM. THE *DIGESTIVE ACIDS* OF THE FISH TEND TO *CORRODE* THE CONTAINERS...

...COMBINING WITH THE *DRUGS* TO CREATE A *UNIQUE* ODOR...

...THAT THE DOG MUST HAVE FOUND *IRRESISTIBLE.*

ONCE BAITED BY THE *SCENT,* HE BOLTED *AWAY* FROM O'SHAUGHNESSY, TORE INTO A *CRATE* AND BEGAN EATING -- HENCE THE *CLAW MARKS* AND TATTERED *BINDINGS.*

THE WORRIED OLD MAN CAME CALLING FOR HIS *PET*... THE *CREW* NO DOUBT CAME UPON THEM *BOTH* AND *PANICKED*...

OFFICER!

AS...YOU... *WISH...!*

1.27

BEFORE WE CAN MOVE A SINGLE **STEP**, THE FLAMES AND THE SMOKE ARE **UPON** US.

AND I KNOW IN THAT ONE MOMENT... THAT I HAVE LOST.

THIS ISN'T A GLASS ROOFTOP. A GRAPPLING LINE WON'T AID ANYONE. SIMON HAD NO WAY TO PREPARE AN OUT.

HE IS TRAPPED HERE, AND HE WILL DIE...DIE HORRIBLY... UNLESS I...

STOP!

"THE MOMENT YOU USE THE POWER THIS BLATANTLY, THIS FORCEFULLY," I WAS WARNED--

"-- THE GAME IS OVER." BY THE TERMS OF MY ASSIGNMENT, I FORFEIT BY HALTING TIME TO ENACT A RESCUE...BUT THERE IS NO ALTERNATIVE THAT WON COST SIMON HIS LIFE.

AND SO, IN THE MOTIONLESS SILENCE OF A FROZEN WORLD, I PONDER AND PLAN...

...ONLY TO HAVE MY CONCENTRATION SHATTERED BY THE IMPOSSIBLE:

1.30

AAAH!

IT ONLY **EASES** THE **PROCESS.**

PROCESS? **WHAT** PROCESS?

OF **TRANSFERENCE.**

DON'T **MISUNDERSTAND,** MISS BISHOP. I HAD NO **INTENTION** OF **INTERRUPTING** YOUR **RESCUE.** IN FACT, I **ENCOURAGE** IT.

I CONFESS I'VE LITTLE **NOTION** WHY YOU'RE SO **RETICENT** TO **WIELD** YOUR POWER... BUT I **ENCOURAGE** YOU TO USE AS MUCH OF IT AS YOU **CARE** TO.

THERE'S NO BETTER WAY FOR ME TO **STEAL** IT.

TO BE CONTINUED

2.2

--I'M HIDING SECRET POWERS FROM YOU RIGHT! THAT I'M NOT ALLOWED TO USE ANYWAY ESPECIALLY IF THIS LEFT! HORRID BARONESS SOMEHOW FILCH RIGHT! THEM FROM ME IF I DO AND WHAT SHE WANTS IS A QUESTION I CAN'T EVEN ASK WITHOUT TIPPING MY HAND AND-- AND--

WELL?

⇒SIGH⇐ YOUR HANDWRITING IS ATROCIOUS.

HOW MONUMENTALLY INFORMATIVE. WITH ACCESS TO DATA LIKE THAT, NO WONDER I'M BRILLIANT.

HOW DO YOU FEEL ABOUT RATS IN LARGE, WRITHING MASSES?

...

WHY?

BECAUSE--

THEY'RE NOT PLAGUE-CARRIERS, HOWEVER. THAT'S A COMMON MISCONCEPTION. IT'S THEIR THOUSANDS OF FLEAS--

I WAS MERELY TRYING TO EASE YOUR MIND.

THOUSANDS OF FLEAS?

OH, THANK YOU!

ON THREE. ONE... TWO...

QUEE SQUEE SQUEE SQUEE SQUEE SQUEE SQUE

2.5

→PFFHTt←

WHY DO *ALL* OUR CASES INVOLVE *RATS* AT ONE POINT OR ANOTHER?

I HADN'T NOTICED.

DO.

SO...TO REVIEW THE *FACTS*...WE LEARNED HOW THE *OPIATES* WERE BEING SMUGGLED INTO PARTINGTON. WE FOUND *METAL PHIALS* SECRETED WITHIN THE CARGO OF *FISH*. WE CRACKED THE *CASE*.

YES. HOW*EVER* WOULD "*WE.*" WE HAVE ESCAPED A *FLAMING BOAT* ABSENT YOUR MASTERY OF *LINGUISTICS*...

NOTHING WAS "*CRACKED.*" I *REMIND* YOU THAT WE CANNOT *TRACE* THE SMUGGLED GOODS TO THEIR *SOURCE* WITHOUT FURTHER *EXAMINING* THEM...

...AND ALL THE DRUG-LADEN *FISH* WERE *DESTROYED* IN THE...

OH! OH, **NO!** SIMON, THERE WERE POLICEMEN ABOARD THE SHIP--!

NOW ON THE **DOCKS.**

PERFECTLY **SAFE.**

PERFECTLY...

→AHEM←

CAUGHT UNDERNEATH YOUR **CLOAK** AS WE THRASHED THROUGH THE **CARGO HOLD,** NO DOUBT.

I ASSUME THIS PUTS US BACK ON THE **TRAIL...?**

XPLOSION...

EMMA? MA, WHY ARE U **SMILING?**

WE'VE SCUSSED MILING.

MISS **BISHOP!** IF YOU'RE SUGGESTING WE--

SIMON... OH, **SIMON...** WHEN I LOOK AT YOU, DO YOU KNOW WHAT I **SEE?**

FISH.

DESPITE SIMON'S IMPATIENT *TOE-TAPPING*, I REPAIR TO MY QUARTERS FOR A QUICK *BATH* AND CHANGE OF *CLOTHING*.

I SUPPOSE I COULD BE MOVING MORE *QUICKLY*, BUT I KNOW WHAT COMES *NEXT*.

VOTES FOR WOMEN

SHRIMP?

NICE. *MOCK* THE *SHORT* MAN.

WHO SAID I WAS REFERRING TO YOUR ENTIRE *BODY?*

DE*LIGHT*FUL. STILL PUTTING THE *"SUFFER"* IN *"SUFFRAGETTE,"* I SEE.

AS DAEDALIAN AS SIMON CAN *BE*, EVEN A HEAD THAT *INFLATED* CAN HOLD ONLY SO MUCH *INFORMATION*.

WHICH IS WHY HE MAINTAINS A WORLDWIDE NETWORK OF *AGENTS -- SPECIALISTS* IN THEIR RESPECTIVE *FIELDS*. *OTTO'S* THE ONLY ONE I'VE EVER MET WHO'S LESS PERSONABLE THAN *SIMON*.

I CAN'T *BELIEVE* WE USED TO *DATE*.

SO I'M SEARCHING FOR ELEMENTS *FORE* TO OUR SHORES.

SOMETHING I CAN TRACE TO A SPECIFIC *REGION* WOULD BE MOST HELPFUL.

CERTAINLY. THERE MUST BE A *TOY SHOPPE* SOMEWHERE IN THE NEIGHBORHOOD.

AND I AM NOT SIMON'S *SCRIVENER!* I AM HIS *PARTNER!*

ASSISTANT.

READ THE *NEWSPAPERS*.

EXAMINE THE *BUSINESS CARDS*.

QUITE THE *CHANGE* FROM YOUR *OLD* PARTNER, SIMON. WHAT WAS HIS *NAME* AGAIN? *LIGHT*SOMETHING...

2.8

TWELVE GALLONS OF *ACID* IN A FOUR-GALLON JAR.

I *HATE* FISH.

OTTO PRESSMONK, ESQ.

CHEMIST

I HATE *CLAMS* AND I HATE *OYSTERS* AND I HATE *COD* AND I HATE--

NOT ASKING FOR MUCH, ARE WE?

FIRST, TO SEPARATE THE DRUG'S *COMPONENTS*. JUST A DRAM OF THERONIUM IODINE...

I THINK YOU MEAN "*IODIDE*."

MY MISTAKE.

HMMM. AN *UNUSUAL* CHAIN OF *FERROUS* MOLECULES...

SIMON, I'LL *BE A* WHILE.

TELL YOUR *SECRETARY* TO COME BY LATER FOR MY *FINDINGS*.

AND ORDER HER TO *REPLACE* MY *CHAIR*.

IGHTBOURNE.

THE WAY SIMON *SPEAKS* IT SPREADS *GOOSEFLESH* ACROSS MY SKIN.

I'VE HEARD RUMORS... *EVERYONE'S* HEARD *RUMORS*... BUT I'VE NEVER ASKED SIMON *DIRECTLY* ABOUT MY PREDECESSOR... OR THE WAY HE *DIED*.

BACK *TO* IT, OTTO. EMMA WILL VISIT YOU AROUND *NOON*.

AND *NO*, I DON'T WISH TO *TALK* ABOUT IT.

ABOUT *WHAT*?

YOU WERE PREPARING TO INQUIRE ABOUT *LIGHTBOURNE*.

YOU *ARE* GOOD.

2.9

ON THE WALK BACK TO HEADQUARTERS, SIMON GROWS INCREASINGLY *REMOTE* AND *WITHDRAWN.*

I DON'T TAKE IT *PERSONALLY,* EVEN AFTER I'M FORCED TO GUIDE HIM BY THE *ELBOW.*

UNDER THOSE RARE CIRCUMSTANCES WHERE SIMON IS *TRULY* PERPLEXED, HE HONES HIS CONCENTRATION BY CLAMBERING INSIDE A BEASTLY CONTRAPTION OF HIS OWN DESIGN--

--A SORT OF *REVERSE BATHYSPHERE* DESIGNED TO DEPRIVE HIM OF *EXTRANEOUS SENSORY INPUT.*

I DO, HOWEVER, WALK HIM THROUGH THE OCCASIONAL *PUDDLE* JUST FOR THE FUN OF IT.

HE CALLS IT HIS *"THINKTANK,"* WHILE I CANCEL HIS *APPOINTMENTS* FOR THE DAY...

...HE PREPARES FOR *IMMERSION.*

HMMM.

CAN'T YOU SLIP INTO A *HOT BATH* LIKE EVERYONE *ELSE*?

SIMON?

WHAT? OH. I WASN'T *LISTENING*.

SHOCKING. YOU KNOW HOW I FEEL ABOUT THAT...THAT *RECEPTACLE*.

YOU'RE *WORRIED* FOR ME.

A BIT.

DO YOU REMEMBER WHAT WE CALL THAT?

"AN EGREGIOUS OUTPOURING OF IRKSOME EMOTION?"

PRECISELY.

WHEN SHALL I SAY YOU'LL BE *AVAILABLE* AGAIN?

WHEN I *AM*.

MEANWHILE, YOU'LL LUNCH WITH THE *COMMISSIONER*?

WITH *PLEASURE*. UNLIKE *SOME* IN YOUR ACQUAINTANCE...

"...HE'S *ALWAYS* GLAD TO SEE ME."

WHAT DO YOU WANT *NOW*?

OH, *MY.* THEOPOLOUS, I APOLOGIZE IF I'VE COME AT AN *INOPPORTUNE TIME...*

NO. NO, IN FACT, I HAVE A MESSAGE OF SOME *IMPORT* FOR YOU *AND* YOUR PARTNER.

AS YOU KNOW, THIS DEPARTMENT HAS TRADITIONALLY EXTENDED TO YOU TWO *EVERY COURTESY.* I, *PERSONALLY,* HAVE CONSIDERED YOU MY *FRIENDS.*

LIKEWISE, THEOP--

NO *MORE.*

... WHAT?

ON HIS *OWN,* WITHOUT AUTHORIZATION, SIMON SIMPLY *COMMANDEERED* A BAND OF *MY OFFICERS* LAST NIGHT!

BUT WITH GOOD *REASON--*

I DON'T *CARE!* IT'S NOT THE *FIRST* TIME HE'S TAKEN *TOTAL LIBERTY* WITH *MY* DEPARTMENT-- BUT IT *IS* THE *LAST!*

DO YOU *HEAR* ME?

EFFECTIVE *IMMEDIATELY,* THERE WILL BE *NO SPECIAL FAVORS* GRANTED BY THIS OFFICE... AND *NO CONSIDERATIONS.*

THEOPOLOUS, THIS DOESN'T *SOUND* LIKE YOU.

THEN PERHAPS YOU NEED A NEW *AUDIOLOGIST.*

I AM THE LAW IN PARTINGTON...

... *NOT* SIMON ARCHARD!

$\mathscr{S}$OMETHING'S NOT RIGHT.

AND SO THE **AFTERNOON.**
WHEREVER I **GO,** A GRUFF
RECEPTION.

ITS AS IF ALL THE MEN
OF **POWER** IN PARTINGTON
ABANDONED THEIR REGARD
FOR SIMON AND HIS
DOINGS **OVERNIGHT.**

OR, RATHER, I SHOULD SAY OVER
NIGHTS...**TWO**...COINCIDING WITH
THE ARRIVAL OF **BARONESS
MIRANDA CROSS** TO OUR CITY...

...AND NO DETECTIVE WORTH A FIG
TAKES **COINCIDENCE** SERIOUSLY.

...AND HOW
WAS SHE ABLE
TO **RESIST** MY
CONTROL?

...IS... MY
GOD...

A DISCREET **CARRIAGE RIDE** BRINGS ME TO HER ESTATE-IN-**PROCESS**--AN ABANDONED CASTLE WHICH CREWS HAVE BEGUN **REFURBISHING** TO HER QUESTIONABLE TASTE.

WHAT DID I EXPECT BY **COMING** HERE? THAT SHE WOULD INVITE ME IN FOR **TEA** SO THAT SHE MIGHT **EXPLAIN** HERSELF...

F SEEMS TO HAVE POWERS TO MATCH OWN...TO EXCEED THEM...BUT **THAT** IS ORMATION I HAVE NO CHOICE BUT TO P **PRIVATE.**

I CANNOT CONFER WITH SIMON ABOUT WHAT I SAW DURING THE **FIRE** WITHOUT REVEALING MY **OWN** SECRETS -- AND I **CANNOT** YET TELL SIMON ABOUT **MY** ABILITIES. I **CAN NOT.** THE **CONSEQUENCES...**

EFORE LAST NIGHT, HE PRICE FOR THEIR SE WAS **FORFEITURE** F ALL I **KNOW.** NOW, PPARENTLY, THE COST S THAT THE BARONESS ILL TAKE THEM FOR ER **OWN**...OR SO SHE AYS...AND, PRESUMABLY, SE THEM **AGAINST** US.

SHE MAY BE **LYING.** BUT FOR **SIMON'S** SAKE, I CANNOT TAKE THAT **RISK.**

WHY WOULD SHE WISH US **HARM?** DID HER PRESENCE ON THE **FISHING BOAT** PROVE A CONNECTION TO ILLICIT **ACTIVITIES?**

AND HOW IS SHE BEHIND THE SUDDEN **SEA CHANGE** IN SIMON'S **POPULARITY?** HOW COULD **ANY** MAN BE INFLUENCED BY A WOMAN WITH SUCH OBVIOUSLY GAUDY AND ECCENTRIC **TASTES?**

WHY, THAT GHASTLY WINDOW **ALONE** IS...

...IS **EVIDENCE.**

I HAVE TO **GO.** I HAVE TO REPORT THIS TO **SIMON...**

...BEFORE I AM **SEEN.**

"I **TOLD** YOU, ANTAEUS..."

2.15

...I CAN HEAR THAT SOW PRACTICALLY *MOOING* WITH FRUSTRATION.

I ALMOST EXPERIENCE A... *PITYING?* IS THAT THE WORD?... PITYING.

AFTER ALL, HER ONLY FUTURE *NOW* LIES IN BECOMING MY FAVORITE *PLAYTHING.*

I'M SORRY, ANTAEUS. MY *SECOND* FAVORITE.

OR *THIRD*, PUTTING *SIMON* IN THE COUNT...

♪ NOW, WHO HERE HAS SOMETHING *FOR ME...?* ♪

USSZZZZ?

YOU ARE MY EYES AND *EARS* IN THIS DREADFUL CITY. GO DO... *THAT.*

NEE*DULLL?*

OH, NO. THERE IS NO *NECESSITY* AT THE *MOMENT* FOR... *DIRECT?*...DIRECT ACTION, YES?

THERE MUST BE *PATIENCE.* THIS, YOU *UNDERSTAND?*

2.16

MY! I *HAVE* HIRED WELL, HAVE I NOT? AN *EMPTY* SYRINGE MEANS YOU'VE ELIMINATED ONE... *SMALL* COMPLICATION FOR US. EXCELLENT.

ALL GOES, ALL GOES. ANTAEUS, FINISH DELIVERING THE LITTLE *BOXES* TO THE *BIG* MEN.

AND TRY NOT TO *BREAK* ANY THIS TIME? IN FACT, *SAVE* YOUR STRENGTH.

GOOD BOYS.

2.17

AS PROMISED, MY RETURN TRIP TAKES ME PAST OTTO'S *LAB* TO RETRIEVE HIS *REPORT*.

Oh...!

THERE WON'T BE ONE.

THE BARONESS. I DON'T KNOW *WHY*, OR *HOW*...

...BUT SHE'S *BEHIND THIS*. I *KNOW IT*.

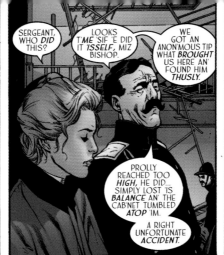

SERGEANT, WHO *DID* THIS?

LOOKS T'ME 'SIF 'E DID IT 'ISSELF, MIZ BISHOP.

WE GOT AN ANON'MOUS TIP WHAT *BROUGHT* US HERE AN' FOUND HIM *THUSLY.*

PROLLY REACHED TOO *HIGH,* HE DID... SIMPLY LOST 'IS *BALANCE* AN' THE CAB'NET TUMBLED *ATOP* 'IM.

A RIGHT UNFORTUNATE *ACCIDENT.*

"ACCIDENT," MY LACE *SHEVIS.*

MYSTER EXPLOSION SINKS VES...

UT BY THE TIME I AKE MY WAY BACK O *47 STRAND* TO ELL SIMON OF MY NDINGS...

SIMON?

SIMON?

SIMON?

...HE'S NOWHERE TO BE *FOUND.*

STILL, OTTO WILL NOT GO *UNAVENGED.* SINCE SIMON LEFT NO NOTE TO THE *CONTRARY,* HE'LL NO DOUBT RETURN *PROMPTLY.*

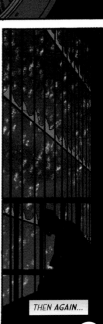

THEN *AGAIN...*

2.19

A DAY LATER, I DON'T KNOW WHETHER TO BE WORRIED FOR OR ANGRY AT SIMON.

WHILE HARDLY A PARAGON OF *WARMTH*, HE'D STILL WANT TO BE *PRESENT* AS WE BURY ONE OF HIS *ASSOCIATES*. THIS, I *KNOW*.

TOO *WELL*.

HAS THE BARONESS ALSO GOTTEN TO *SIMON* SOMEHOW, WITHOUT DISCLOSING HER TRIUMPH TO *ME*?

I DOUBT IT. JUDGING BY HER BEHAVIOR AT *THE FIRE*, SHE'D WANT ME TO *KNOW*.

NO *AUTOPSY* WAS NECESSARY. THE AUTHORITIES, FRANKLY, COULDN'T *WAIT* TO GET OTTO INTO THE *GROUND*. BLESS HIS SOUL, HE COUNTED AMONG HIS COMPATRIOTS ONLY A HANDFUL OF SIMON'S FELLOW *OPERATIVES*. BARTLESBY THE MOUCH... THE ABBESS *LADYBIRD NELL*... A FEW OTHERS...

...HARDLY A FITTING *FUNEREAL PARTY* FOR EVEN A MAN OF OTTO'S SOUR DISPOSITION. IF HE HAD ANY *FAMILY*...

--GATHERED HERE T PAY *FINAL RESPECTS* THE DECEASED --

HAD T'GO HEARIN' ABOUT THIS IN THE *PENNYSHEETS*, Y'BLOODY *SHORTWANK*...

...LEF' ME QUITE ITCH T'SCR WI' YE, BR(OTTO...

THE *DEAD*? THERE AIN'T NO WORDS *FOUL* ENOUGH. YE THINK YERSELVES HIS *FRIENDS*? NO.

THAT'S WHAT I KEEP *TELLING* MYSELF.

...I'D BE *AMAZED*.

--A SOUL *RELEASED* FROM THIS MORTAL COIL TO BATHE IN THE LIGHT OF --

...LEAVIN' OUR *MUM* WI'OUT TWO COINS T'RUB *TOGETHER* F'R EVEN TH' *WARMTH* OF IT...

...YER *NIECES* 'N' *NEPHEWS* ALLUS IGNORED THO' I *BEGS* YE T'PUT *FOOD* IN THEIR HUNGRY MOUTHS...

MADAM, OUR *CONDOLENCES*. WE HAD *NO IDEA* OTTO HAD A *SISTER*...

...BUT *REGARDLESS* OF WHATEVER QUARRELS YOU *KNEW*, THE TWO OF YOU, WE *IMPLORE* YOU TO SPEAK NO ILL OF THE... THE...

THESE ARE ALL WHAT'S FIT T'SHARE THEIR TIME WI' *OTTO PRESSMONK!*

LET THE *MAGGOTS* BE WITH THEIR *OWN!*

OH, GOOD *LORD!* GET THEM *OFF!* *GET THEM OFF!*

2.21

WHILE THE ABBESS AND THE PRIEST RELIEVE THEMSELVES OF THE CONTENTS OF THEIR **STOMACHS**, WE TRY OUR **BEST** TO SALVAGE OTTO'S **DIGNITY**...

...BUT THERE ARE TOO **MANY** OF THE WRIGGLING LARVAE... AND THEY'LL FIND OTTO SOONER THAN LATER, **ANYWAY**. WITH GRIEF MORE PROFOUND THAN **BEFORE**, WE EASE OTTO INTO THE **EARTH**... AND SING A **PRAYER** THOUGH WE'RE ONE VOICE **SHORT**.

SIMON...

...WHERE ARE YOU

CONTINUED NEXT ISSUE

I COULD HAVE TAKEN A CARRIAGE BACK FROM OTTO'S FUNERAL.

I ELECT TO WALK.

IT'LL DULL THE IMPULSE TO BURY SIMON RIGHT *NEXT* TO HIM.

EVEN THOUGH SIMON ARCHARD HURTLES THROUGH LIFE WITH THE COMPASSION OF A *THROWN BRICK*, IT'S *UNFORGIVABLE* THAT HE WOULD *IGNORE* A MEMORIAL SERVICE FOR ONE OF HIS *OWN OPERATIVES*.

IT'S NOT AS IF SIMON'S MET WITH FOUL PLAY *HIMSELF*. IF *THAT* WERE THE CASE, I WOULD HAVE... BEEN *NOTIFIED*.

BUT EVEN IF HE'S DOGMATICALLY FOLLOWING A NEW LEAD ON THE *OPIATE SMUGGLING* CASE, NOTHING--AND I MEAN *NOTHING*-- KEEPS SIMON FROM *DEVOURING* THE WARES OF THE *CORNER NEWS VENDORS*.

SIMON *PRIDES* HIMSELF ON STAYING INFORMED ON ALL MATTERS REGARDING THE CITY OF PARTINGTON--AND OTTO'S *DEATH* HEADLINED *EVERY BROADSHEET*.

WHICH BRINGS US BACK TO "UNFORGIVABLE."

HOWEVER, ONCE I LAY EYES ON *47 STRAND* ONCE MORE...

...SUDDENLY, BEATING AN *EXCUSE* OUT OF SIMON IS THE *LAST* THING ON MY MIND.

AS IT HAPPENS, WHILE I'VE BEEN BUSY CONDEMNING *SIMON*...

3.1

...SOMEONE *ELSE* HAS BEEN CONDEMNING HIS *HEADQUARTERS*.

WHAT THE *DEVIL*...?

OFFICER, WHAT'S THE *MEANING* OF THIS?

MISS *BISHOP*, IS IT? MISS BISHOP, WE'LL HAVE *NAE TROUBLE* HERE FROM THE LIKES O' *YOU*.

"THE *LIKES OF*..."?

WAIT. OVER *THERE*. THE MEN GIVING THE *ORDERS* --

-- THEY'RE THE *MAYOR* OF PARTINGTON -- AND THE *BANKER*, WHO --

--*DECONSECRATED* OR *NOT, NEVER* SHOULD HAVE SOLD SUCH A *SACRED BUILDING* TO SUCH A *PROFANE MARPLOT*! MY MOST SINCERE *APOLOGIES*, MAYOR!

I *AGREE* IT'S A *SIN* TO SEE THIS CATHEDRAL GO FROM *NO USE* TO *ILL* USE, PERTHANBY --

-- AND I'M *INCLINED* SIMPLY TO BURN IT TO THE *GROUND* TO ALLEVIATE THE STINK OF *HERESY* FROM ITS *RAFTERS*!

YOU *HEARD* ME, MISS BISHOP!

BOTH OF THESE MEN HAVE ALWAYS BEEN STAUNCH *SUPPORTERS* OF SIMON'S ACTIVITIES. THEIR SUDDEN *TURNABOUT* PERPLEXES ME...

...UNTIL I SEE THEM DIP *SNUFF* FROM BOXES OF A CHILLINGLY FAMILIAR *DESIGN*...

3.2

ONE THAT MARKS THEM AS *GIFTS* OM THE BARONESS *MIRANDA CROSS*... *PORTER* OF THE OPIATE HIDDEN IN THE UFF...A DRUG WHICH APPARENTLY ALLOWS R SOME MEASURE OF *CONTROL* OVER OSE WHO *PARTAKE* OF IT.

AND WHERE, DEAR GIRL, *IS* YOUR EMPLOYER? I WAS LOOKING *FORWARD* TO *PERSONALLY* RUNNING HIM OUT OF *TOWN*...

...WITH *YOU* NOT FAR *BEHIND!*

I *ASSURE* YOU, MAYOR, I'VE NO MORE IDEA WHERE MY

PARTNER

IS THAN DO *YOU*...

...BUT AS THIS IS THE MOST LOGICAL SITE FOR HIS *RETURN*, I'VE *EVERY RIGHT* AS A *LAW-ABIDING CITIZEN* TO WAIT FOR HIM *HERE*.

IF YOU WISH ME TO *LEAVE*, YOU'LL HAVE TO *PHYSICALLY REMOVE* ME FROM --

--*OH!*

THIS WAY, MISSY. AND STOP *SQUIRMING*.

I HAVE A TOUCH OF THE *SCIATICA*.

3.3

SCIATICA?

IT'S A PINCHED NERVE COND—

I KNOW WHAT SCIATICA IS, YOU OX! PUT ME DOWN!

WITH PLEASURE.

SHE'S ALL *YOURS*, BOSS.

ENJOY.

"WHERE HAVE YOU *BEEN?*"

"CERTAINLY, *SOMEONE'S* BEHIND OUR CURRENT DIFFICULTIES."

"WHERE HAVE YOU *BEEN?*"

"THE BARONESS IS AS VIABLE A *SUSPECT* AS *ANY*."

"WHERE HAVE YOU *BEEN?*"

"PARTICULARLY SINCE SHE AND THE *OPIATE* HIT OUR SHORES *SIMULTANEOUSLY*."

"*WHERE HAVE YOU BEEN?*"

...

OUT.

WHAT HAVE YOU *LEARNED?*

THAT YOU'RE A *HORSE'S ARSE*. ALSO NOT *NEWS*.

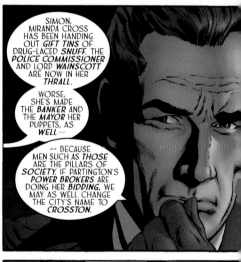

SIMON, MIRANDA CROSS HAS BEEN HANDING OUT *GIFT TINS* OF DRUG-LACED *SNUFF*. THE *POLICE COMMISSIONER* AND LORD *WAINSCOTT* ARE NOW IN HER *THRALL*.

WORSE, SHE'S MADE THE *BANKER* AND THE *MAYOR* HER PUPPETS, AS *WELL*—

—BECAUSE MEN SUCH AS *THOSE* ARE THE PILLARS OF *SOCIETY*. IF PARTINGTON'S *POWER BROKERS* ARE DOING HER *BIDDING*, WE MAY AS WELL CHANGE THE CITY'S NAME TO *CROSSTON*.

NO!

SIMON, *NO!* THAT WAS *YOU?* IN DISGUISE?

THAT OTTO WAS *MURDERED*, I HAVE NO *DOUBT*.

BUT SINCE WE'RE BEING LED TO BELIEVE *OTHERWISE*, I CHOSE TO KEEP MY INVESTIGATION *LOW-PROFILE*.

I WOULDN'T *COUNT* ON IT, BARONESS! YES, I *KNOW* IT'S *YOU!*

AND I *SWEAR* TO YOU BY ALL THAT IS *HOLY* THAT YOU WILL DERIVE *NO PLEASURE* FROM MY *PRESENCE!*

THIS IS *NEWS?*

I'M *OVERPAYING* YOU.

TAP TAP

SIMON!

OF COURSE. NOW...

...WHAT'S THIS ABOUT THE *BARONESS MIRANDA...?*

...WISH THIS CAME AS LESS OF A ...VELATION TO YOU. I *ASSUMED* ...U WERE *INVESTIGATING* THIS ...RY NOTION. *THAT* WOULD BE YOUR *ONLY* EXCUSE FOR ...MISSING OTTO'S *FUNERAL.*

IT WAS *BLEAK* AND *HORRIBLE,* SIMON. SOME ...OLD *CRONE* EVEN THREW A FISTFUL OF--OF--

MAGGOTS?

YES! *MAGGOTS* INTO THE *COFFIN* AND--

--WAIT. HOW DID YOU KNOW *THAT?*

BECAUSE THEY TOOK ALL *NIGHT* TO GATHER.

SO WHAT HAVE *YOU* LEARNED?

NOTHING.

YET.

THAT'S WHAT THE *MAGGOTS* ARE FOR.

AND...? THAT CRIES *OUT* FOR EXPLANATION!

YOU WON'T LIKE IT.

LET ME BE THE JUDGE OF--

→SNIFF← →SNIFF←

SIMON, IS THAT *CAMPHOR?*

YES. I'VE SPREAD SOME UNDER MY NOSE. I SUGGEST YOU DO THE SAME.

WHY?

3.5

3.6

POSSIBLY.

3.8

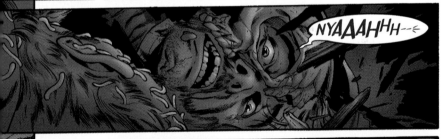

NOT ALL OF SIMON'S OPERATIVES ARE ON A **PAYROLL**. MANY OF TH... LESS FREQUENTLY **CONSULTED**-- PARTICULARLY THOSE WHO ARE WELL- TO-DO **THEMSELVES**--LEND THEIR SERVICES IN EXCHANGE FOR PAST FA...

HEADMASTER **WARREN SUMMERSBY** O... **PARTINGTON UNIVERSITY**, FOR EXAMP...

AT SIMON'S BEHEST, SUMMERSBY KEEP... WATCH OVER HIS BEST AND BRIGHTES... STUDENTS WITH AN EYE TOWARDS WHICH ONES MAY, IN TIME, BECOME EITHER **ALLIES** OR **ADVERSARIES**.

THE DAMAGE TO OTTO'S **BODY** WAS **INCONSISTENT** WITH THE SIZE OF THE SHELF THAT "FELL" ON HIM. SINCE THERE WAS NO **AUTOPSY** AND OTTO WAS, FOLLOWING HIS PROCLAIMED WISHES, BURIED **SANS ENBALMING**...

...THE MAGGOTS WERE MY WAY OF LEECHING ENOUGH FLUID FROM OTTO'S **SYSTEM** TO DETERMINE IF HE WAS **POISONED** RATHER THAN **CRUSHED**.

AND HE **WAS**.

MOREOVER, THE LARVAE AND THIS **SMUGGLED PHIAL** TEST CONSISTENTLY WITH EACH **OTHER**. THIS INDICATES THAT OTTO WAS INJECTED WITH A FATAL DOSE OF THE VERY OPIATE THE BARONESS IS USING TO MANIPULATE HER **VICTIMS**.

ASTOUNDING.

OTTO **CONTINUES** TO AID US FROM BEYOND THE **GRAVE**. HE--

AVAILED NEITHER OF *OTTO'S* LABORATORY NOR HIS *OWN*, SIMON ASKS FOR AND IS GRANTED TEMPORARY ACCESS TO THE *SCHOOL'S* FACILITIES, BUT...

...WE HAVEN'T MUCH *TIME*. THE *STUDENTS* WILL ARRIVE SHORTLY, AND I'D RATHER NOT HAVE TO DEAL WITH THEIR *FAWNING ADMIRATION*. IT'S QUITE THE *NUISANCE*.

WHAT?

NOTHING.

AAAAH! MON, THEY'RE *FLYING--!*

TKK
KK
TKK
TKK
TKK TKK TKK TKK
TKK TKK TKK
TKK

NO. NO, THEY'RE *CLINGING* TO THE *METAL RIM* OF THE *MAGNIFYING LENS.*

THE *DRUG...* MADE THEM... *MAGNETIC?* THAT'S --

FASCINATING.

I WAS GOING TO SAY *"REVOLTING"*... BUT HOW DOES THAT FIT IN WITH THIS NOTION OF *MENTAL CONTROL?*

WE'LL ASK *ADELINE.*

HOW MANY *OPERATIVES* DO YOU *HAVE...?*

3.11

...AND DISTRACT HER *MOTHER* WHILE I ARRANGE A *CONFERENCE*.

DISTRACT? HOW? I DON'T EVEN *KNOW* THE WOMAN!

YOU'RE *THEATRICAL.* YOU'LL THINK OF SOMETHING.

SPLENDID.

LISTEN FOR *TWO THUMPS.*

TWO WHAT?

"...YOUR GUIDE TO THE REALM ECTOPLATHMIC!"

I'M *THORRY,* MITH WINKLE! WOULD YOU LIKE ME TO POUR YOU THOME *TEA,* FIRTHY?

"AND A *THCONE,* IF YOU WILL?"

THERTAINLY. NOW EVERYONE CONTHENTRAIL...

"THPEAK, OH DEARLY DEPARTED OF THE THPIRIT WORLD! WHAT METHAGE DO YOU HAVE FOR UTH TODAY...?"

BEWA... OF T... *SCON...*

Oh, I *THOUGHT* I HEARD SOMEONE OUTSIDE. MAY I *HELP* YOU?

...

YES. YES, I'M... ADELINE'S...

...*TEACHER*.

MY ADELINE? SHE'S *HOME SCHOOLED!*

AND BY *"TEACHER,"* I MEAN HER *MUSIC* TEACHER.

SHE PLAYS NO *INSTRUMENTS.*

SHE *SINGS* FOR ME.

SHE HAS A VOICE LIKE *GRAVEL.*

EXACTLY. MAY I COME IN? THENKYEW...

I DON'T....

⇒SIGH⇐

SHE'S UPSTAIRS. SHALL I *SUMMON* HER?

GRACIOUS, *NO!* LEAVE THE DEAR TO HER *PLAYTHINGS*...

"JOIN HANDTH, MY FRIENDTH! MADAM TREBLINKA WILL BE YOUR *GUIDE* TODAY..."*

YOU'LL *FORGIVE* ME, DEAR, BUT YOU LOOK A *FRIGHT.*

Oh, I *KNOW.* *RUFFIANS. THREE* OF THEM. ATTEMPTED TO *MUG* ME JUST *OUTSIDE.*

MY *WORD!* IN *THIS* NEIGHBORHOOD?

I AM *FINDING* THESE DAYS, MA'AM, THAT INIQUITY AND PERNICIOUSNESS HIDE IN THE MOST *UNLIKELY* OF VENUES.

POOR THING. NOW, ABOUT THESE *VOICE LESSONS*... YOU SAY MY *HUSBAND* APPROACHED YOU ON *ADDIE'S* BEHALF? THAT DOESN'T SOUND LIKE HIM AT *ALL.*

WELL... YOU KNOW HOW HE CAN *BE.*

Ah. SO TRUE... SO *TRUE.*

WHEW.

3.13

THIMON. THAT WATH *YOU.*

THAT WATH *MEAN!*

WE'VE *MET*, HAVEN'T WE?

BY THE WAY, IF YOU WERE *TRULY* A PSYCHIC, YOU WOULD HAVE *PREDICTED* MY ARRIVAL.

MAGNETIC OR TOPOGRAPHICAL?

MAGNETIC.

OKAY. THE WHOLE *PLANET* ITH RINGED WITH THEM. THEY'RE *IRREGULAR*, BUT ONE RUNTH THRAIGHT THROUGH *PARTINGTON.* IT'TH *VERY* POWERFUL.

NOW, SUPPOSING A MAN'S *BRAIN* WERE *LACED* WITH PARTICLES *SENSITIVE* TO THAT MAGNETISM.

WHAT WOULD THAT *DO* TO HIM?

Hmm... ADDIE?

I'M *THINKING.* BUT *HE* MIGHT NOT BE ABLE TO, AT LEATHT NOT *RATIONALLY.*

DEPENDING ON HOW MUCH HE HAD IN HIM, THE *MAGNETITHM* WOULD *THERTAINLY* ALTER THE BRAIN'TH *ELECTROMAGNETIC* FIELD.

THANK YOU, ADELINE. YOU MAY RETURN TO YOUR *DOLLIES* AND THEIR EXPLORATION INTO THE *METAPHYSICAL.*

AS USUAL, IT MIGHT BE BEST IF YOUR MOTHER HAD NO *KNOWLEDGE* OF MY VISIT.

AREN'T YOU AFRAID OF HER *WALKING IN?*

I AM *TOO* PTHYCHIC. YOU'RE ATH BAD ATH *MOMMY*.

YOU'VE *THEEN* WHAT I CAN *DO*, THIMON. I FOUND THE *GHOTHT OF MARPON LANE* FOR YOU!

WE'VE GONE *OVER* THIS, ADELINE. THERE'S NO SUCH *THING* AS GHOSTS.

Heh.

WHAT YOU *EXPERIENCE* WHEN YOU GO INTO A SELF-HYPNOTIC *STATE--*

TRANTH.

--IS AN INCREASED ELECTROMAGNETIC PERCEPTION OF SOME AS-YET-UNNAMED *ENERGY.*

THAT'S WHY I'VE COME TO YOU, *TODAY,* IN FACT. TELL ME...

...HAVE YOU ANY EXPERIENCE WITH *LEY LINES*?

NO.

THUMP THUMP

HEAVENS! WHAT'S THAT *RACKET*? ADDIE?

ADELINE BETHESMA DEWINTER! WHAT HAVE YOU GOTTEN INTO *NOW*?

ANSWER ME!

AND *THAT--*

--IS MY CUE TO *LEAVE.* WHAT AN *ORDEAL.*

STILL, IT MIGHT BE *WORTH* IT IF I CAN SEE SIMON SHINNY DOWN A *DRAINPIPE...*

3.17

ANTAEUS, LOOK WHO IT IS!

BRINDROD'S GUANO SHOVEL CO.

SIMON, DON'T MAKE A *SCENE...!*

YOU NEEDN'T *WARN* ME AS IF I WERE A *SCHOOLCHILD,* EMMA.

I'M *NOT* WARNING HIM. *I*'M *PROTECTING* HIM.

I AND *I* ALONE *KNOW* THAT THE BARONESS POSSESSES *SORCEROUS ABILITIES* THE LIMITS OF WHICH I'VE NOT *SEEN TESTED.* I'VE WITNESSED THEM WITH MY *OWN EYES.*

PLEASE TO MAKE NO FURTHER *EXCUSES* FOR *IGNORING* ME, DEAR MAN. YOU *PROMISED* TO COME BY AND PERUSE THE COLLECTION OF *CLIPPINGS* I HAVE ASSEMBLED REGARDING YOUR... *EXPLOITS,* YES?

I FEAR, HOWEVER, THAT THE BARONESS WOULD *GLADLY* EXPOSE US *BOTH* IF IT MEANT SPURRING ME TO *ACTION.*

SUBTEXT? YOU MEAN YOU REALLY AREN'T *AWARE,* SIMON? WOULD YOU CARE FOR AN *EDUCATION?*

SIMON KNOWS *ALL* HE *NEEDS* TO KNOW ABOUT *YOU,* BARONESS.

I HIGHLY *DOUBT* THAT. WHY, THERE ARE ALL *SORTS* OF SECRETS LURKING UNDER SIMON'S VERY *NOSE.* FOR *INSTANCE*--

SIMON, WE'RE WASTING VALUABLE *TIME* HERE. LET'S GO.

NOT **DISCLOSED**
CAPABILITIES TO
ON, NOR DO I
H TO. NOT ONLY
ULD I HAVE TO
HIS **SKEPTICISM**--

UT TO **TELL**
WOULD BE
ADMIT I HAVE
TAIN...**POWERS**
F MY **OWN**--

BARONESS,
EMOVE YOUR HANDS
OM MY PARTNER, OR I
LL REMOVE THEM **FOR**--

--POWERS THE BARONESS
PROMISED TO **THIEVE** FROM
ME THE NEXT TIME THEY'RE
USED. I CANNOT EVEN **TOUCH**
HER WITHOUT RISKING A VERY
TELLING DISPLAY OF **ENERGY**.

-- YOU.

TROUBLE, EMMA, DARLING?
FEEL **FREE** TO...I BELIEVE THE
PHRASE IS, "PUT ME IN
MY **PLACE**."

ONLY
AS **I** SEE FIT,
MIRANDA.

BEGGING
YOUR **PARDON**,
BUT WOULD YOU
TWO PLEASE **REPEAT**
THAT EXCHANGE? I
CAN BARELY **HEAR** IT
OVER THE CLAMOR
OF **MYSTERIOUS
SUBTEXT**.

ED NO **CROCODILE TEARS**
MY **DEPARTURE**, BARONESS.
EL QUITE **CONFIDENT** THAT
R PATHS WILL INTERWEAVE
QUITE SOON.

IN THE MEANTIME,
OU'LL HAVE TO BE
ONTENT WITH YOUR
CLIPPINGS.

Oh, I **SHALL**. IN
FACT, ANTAEUS HAS
FOUND YET **MORE**
NEWS REGARDING
THE GREAT SIMON
ARCHARD...

...FRESH
OFF THE
PRESS.

The PENNY ARCADIAN
Copiously Illustrated   Afternoon Edition, Price One Penny

FAMED DETECTIVE
MURDERS GRAND DAME
MON ARCHARD SLAYS LADY PENELOPE WAINSCOT
ANDSOME BOUNTY OFFERED

3.19

THE LADY WAINSCOTT? BUT THAT'S NOT--

TRUE? IT'S QUITE *FULL* OF *ONE* TRUTH.

THAT SHE WOULD, OF *COURSE*, HAVE *MURCHISON* AS WELL. COME ALONG, EMMA...

"...THINGS ARE ABOUT TO GET *MUCH WORSE*"

THAT'S *HIM!*

I *SEE* 'IM!

ALLUS *FIGGERED* HE'D TURN SOMEDAY, I DID.

POLICE! *POLICE!*

GRA_ HIM.

Ohhh--! THE *MONSTER!*

HOY, NOW! I'LL GET HIM! I GOT A *FINE REWARD* RUNNIN' RIGHT *TOWARDS* ME!

WAINSCOTT *MANOR?*

SIMON, HAVE YOU TAKEN LEAVE OF YOUR *SENSES?* PERHAPS THE ALLEGED *CRIME SCENE* ISN'T THE BEST PLACE TO *BE AT THE MOMENT...?*

AS OPPOSED TO WHERE *ELSE?* BESIDES, THIS PLACE WILL BE *TEEMING* WITH CLUES THAT WILL *EXPOSE* THIS PATHETIC FRAME, EMMA.

I DOUBT THE *BODY* IS STILL HERE, BUT--

--BUT I COULD BE *WRONG!* LADY WAINSCOTT!

SIMON? *ELLA?*

THIS IS AN UNEXPECTED SURPRISE! WHAT BRINGS THE TWO OF *YOU* HERE?

UUULLPP--!

CLIMB *IN!* HURRY!

IF THE *COMMISSIONER* IS MIRANDA'S PUPPET AS *WELL*, THEN HIS *OFFICERS* ARE DOUBTLESS CONVERGING ON US EVEN AS WE--

CONGRATULATIONS. USE IT TO BUY A NEW *CAB.*

FWEEEEEEE

HE'S GETTIN' *AWAY!* AFTER 'IM!

YOU DO. YOU'RE IN *DEADLY DANGER*, AGATHA -- MOST LIKELY FROM YOUR *OWN HUSBAND.* WHERE *IS* HE?

I WISH I *KNEW*, DEAR. I COULD HAVE *SWORN* HE SAID HE WAS GOING INTO TOWN FOR SOME *SNUFF*, BUT I MUST HAVE *MISHEARD.*

I FOUND QUITE AN *ABUNDANCE* IN THE *GIFT BOX* THE BARONESS SENT HIM.

THAT'S RIGHT. DON'T BREATHE A *WORD*, DEAR SIMON, BUT THIS OLD BIDDY ENJOYS A PINCH OR TWO *HERSELF* FROM TIME TO --

NEEEEEE!

AGATHA!

3.21

4.1

OF COURSE. WHAT I *GLIMPSED*, *YOU* COMMITTED TO *MEMORY*. WELL *DONE*. THEN YOU *KNOW* THE TRUE PATH.

AN INTERESTING CHOICE OF WORDS. I MIGHT HAVE GONE WITH, *"DEAR LORD, WE HAVEN'T A PRAYER!",* BUT THAT'S JUST *ME*.

I WAS AFFORDED A *BRIEF GLANCE* FROM *ABOVE* AS WE CROSSED THE *REAR PATIO*, SIMON. I *THINK* WE TAKE OUR NEXT *LEFT--*

NO.

NO.

AH. AND JUST WHEN I THOUGHT IT WAS *HOPELESS...*

THIS MIGHT BE A GOOD TIME FOR YOU TO REMOVE YOUR *SCARF*.

WHY ON *EARTH--?*

*PROPH*ECIES...

FINE.

NOW FIND A *STONE*.

WH--

FINE.

YES. THAT'S CORRECT. THE IMMUTABLE LAWS OF *PHYSICAL GEOMETRY* HAVE *SHATTERED* LIKE A *GLAZED TEACUP* BEFORE OUR *VERY EYES* AND WE ARE POSITIVELY *DOOMED*.

DEAR LORD, WE REALLY HAVEN'T A...

...

WHAT?

4.4

IT'S SO PAINFULLY *SIMPLE* AN OBSERVATION, EMMA, THAT IT OFTEN *ESCAPES* EVEN THE MOST *ARDENT* PUZZLE MAVEN.

THERE IS A *SECRET* TO NAVIGATING LABYRINTHS, AND IT IS *THIS*: NO MATTER THEIR *COMPLEXITY*, FROM ENTRANCE TO EXIT...

...THEY ARE NO MORE AND NO LESS *ONE LONG LINE*, BROKEN ONLY BY GAPS FOR *ENTRANCE* AND *EGRESS*.

THEREFORE... AS, THANKFULLY, *NO* CONSTABULARY REALIZE...

WHOK

...AND ALL THAT MAY LIE *BEYOND.*

*S*IMON, NATURALLY, IS RIGHT. THE BARONESS IS NO LONGER **TOYING** WITH US. CLEARLY, IF SHE'S FRAMED SIMON FOR **MURDER,** SHE NEEDS US DECISIVELY OUT OF HER WAY.

LIGHT THE *FIRE,* ANTAEUS.

AND WITH IT, LIGHT THE *FUTURE...*

...FOR TOMORROW'S *DAWN* WILL BRING A *NEW DAY* TO THE CITY OF PARTINGTON.

OR A NEW *NIGHT.* OR A NEW *GLOOM.* OR A *FISCAL PANIC* OR *CRIME SPREE* OR A *THUNDERSHOWER* OF *TOAD CORPSES* SLICKING THE SIDEWALKS AND COBBLESTONES IF I AM SO DESIRING.

I KNOW. YOU NEEDN'T SAY IT. *FICKLE* IN MY *AMUSEMENTS,* I AM.

AFTER *TONIGHT,* I WILL HOL THIS CITY IN MY *HAN* ANTAEUS, ALLOW ME FORMALLY INTRODU YOU TO ITS *FINGERS.*

THE NEXT TIME COMMISIONER THORNTON DISPATCHES A MAN TO COVER AN *EXIT*...

...HE'D BE WISE TO CHOOSE ONE WITH A *THICKER SKULL*.

COME ALONG. WE HAVEN'T MUCH *TIME*.

MY SUGGESTION THAT WE LAY *LOW* IS MET WITH A GRAND ROLLING OF SIMON'S *EYES*. INSTEAD, THROUGHOUT THE REST OF THE AFTERNOON, SIMON MAKES SURE WE'RE SEEN STEALING *CARRIAGES*, HAUNTING THE *RAILWAY STATION*, AND DELVING INTO THE *CITY SEWERS*. (AGAIN WITH THE *RATS. LOVELY.*)

IT'S A GAMBIT *WELL-PLAYED*. BY *EVENING*, EVERY NEWSPAPER IN *TOWN* REPORTS THAT SIMON (AND HIS "ACCOMPLICE ELLE BISHOP"--I SIMPLY *MUST* CONTRACT A *PUBLICITY AGENT*) ARE MAKING EVERY EFFORT TO *FLEE* PARTINGTON FOR LANDS *UNKNOWN.* THE BARONESS HAS GOTTEN HER *WAY.*

OR *HAS* SHE...?

IAN PERTHABY, PARTINGTON'S RICHEST *BANKER*...

...AUBREGINE *WAINSCOTT*, ITS MOST INFLUENTIAL *BUSINESSMAN* AND ⇒TCH⇐ RECENT *WIDOWER*...

...MAYOR *CHARLESTON BULLROND*...

...POLICE COMMISSIONER *THEOPOLOUS THORNTON*...

4.7

DING DONG

...AND THAT WOULD BE MAKING *FIVE.*

NOT *YET.*

MRFFT?

BECAUSE THE IDENTITY OF MIRANDA'S *FINAL* GUEST SHOULD BE *MOST* OBVIOUS. WHO ELSE BUT...

CLIPPINGS...

CNNN BRRTH.

NEVER MIND. IT'S AS I *SUSPECTED.* MIRANDA HAS THE TOWN FATHERS *GORGONIZED,* AND SHE'S ONLY JUST *BEGINNING* HER MACHINATIONS.

CNNN BRRTH.

EXACTLY. HOW TO *STOP* IT?

CNNN BRRTH.

AGREED. ADELINE WAS *RIGHT.* BUT HOW BEST TO DEAL WITH THE *FIRE?*

CNNN BRRTH!

CNNNNN'T BREATHE, I SAI--

⇒HEFF⇐ THANK YOU.

"HIDE IN THERE, EMMA. YOU'LL BE FINE."

SIMON, WHAT'S *HAPPENING?*

4.8

EDITOR RANDOLPH MURCHISON, THE INK OF THE *PENNY ARCADIAN* STILL *WET* BENEATH HIS *MANICURE.* DO ENTER FREELY AND WITHOUT *FEAR,* DEAR SIR.

YOU HAVE *BRINGED...* NO, *BROUGHT...* BROUGHT A LITTLE SOMETHING *EXTRA* FOR ME, HAVE YOU?

AS YOU *REQUESTED,* BARONESS MIRANDA. MORE *NEWSPAPER CLIPPINGS* FOR YOUR *COLLECTION.*

SHEAVES OF NEWSPRINT FROM *FOREIGN SHORES* REGARDING THE *SLEUTH* --

-- WHO IS BEST LEFT SPOKEN OF SOME *OTHER* DAY. COME ALONG. MUCH TO *DO...*

"NOTHING *GOOD,* THE *NARCOTICS* MIRANDA'S BEEN IMPOSING ON THOSE FIVE MEN, WHEN CARRIED THROUGH THE BLOODSTREAM TO THE *BRAIN,* DEPOSIT *FERROUS TRACES* TO CREATE A *MAGNETIC PULSE.*

"THAT *PULSE,* WHEN ATTUNED TO THE *LEY LINES* RUNNING THROUGH PARTINGTON, APPARENTLY ALLOWS MIRANDA A CERTAIN MEASURE OF *HYPNOTIC CONTROL* OVER THOSE SO *TAINTED...*

"...A MEASURE SHE MEANS THIS NIGHT TO *PERMANENTLY STRENGTHEN* BY FEEDING HER SUBJECTS *MORE* OF THE DRUG *HERE*...AROUND THAT ODD *BLUE FLAME...*

"...THE VERY SPOT WHERE PARTINGTON'S MAGNETIC LEYS *CONVERGE.*"

4.9

...*REALLY* SHOULD HAVE OPENED MY *OWN* DETECTIVE AGENCY...

NO *WORRIES*, SIMON. →*NNGH*← THE *FLOOR* BROKE MY *FALL*. TAPESTRIES DON'T WELL HOLD THE WEIGHT OF *ARMORED SUITS*, YOU KNOW.

SIMON, I COULD POSITIVELY *KILL* YOU AT THIS MOMENT --

YOU'LL *FORGIVE* ME...

...BUT THAT JOB HA BEEN *TAKEN*, YO OVEROFFICIO *HAYBAG.*

KRAK

NNNGH!

YOU... LUMBERING... *BRUTE.* CAN YOU EVEN...*SEE* YOUR FEET FROM WAY UP THERE?

THAT'S... WHAT I *THOUGHT.*

AS I RECALL, YOU HAVE SOME MAGIC OF YOUR *OWN*. FEEL *FREE* TO EXPLOIT IT TO ITS *UTMOST*.

IT WILL NOT *SAVE* YOU.

FWOOM

EMMA! *THIS* WAY! WE MUST TEND TO THE *FIRE!* WE--

→HRRGGH!←

KILL ARCHARD.

KILL ARCHARD.

KILL ARCHARD.

KILL ARCHARD.

KILL ARCHARD.

4.13

BY ADDING FUEL.

PERFECT, THERE YOU GO, SIMON. IN THE NICK OF TIME, I TWIST AWAY--

--FOR IN THAT HALF-SECOND, THE ONLY LIGHT IN THE **WORLD** IS **BLUE**--

HOW **DARE** YOU **STRIKE** **ME?**

--AS MIRANDA'S WRATH TURNS THE **BONFIRE** INTO A **RAGING INFERNO!**

4.17

4.18

"BRILLIANTLY *PLAYED*, EMMA!"

"EMMA, ARE YOU ALL RIGHT?"

"EMMA, ARE YOU ALL RIGHT?"

YOU WEIGH MORE THAN I *THOUGHT.*

YOU'RE *WELCOME...*

GOOD *LORD...SO HOT...!*

AS A TRAINED *DETECTIVE*, I ATTRIBUTE THAT TO THE *FIRE.* LET'S ESCAPE WHILE WE *CAN.*

WAIT! THE *MEN--!*

--ARE EXPERIENCING A SUDDEN *CLARITY.*

THIS WAY!

SIMON *ARCHARD?* WHAT AM I --

-- WHAT ARE *WE* DOING *HERE?*

YOU'VE *FREED* THEM FROM MIRANDA'S *GRASP?*

I DIDN'T. THE *FIRE* DID.

INTENSE HEAT *WEAKENS* MAGNETIC FIELDS *SEVERELY.*

ONLY BY TURNING THE CEREMONIAL PYRE INTO A *GRAND CONFLAGRATION* COULD I *HOPE* TO WAKE MIRANDA'S VICTIMS FROM THEIR *ELECTROMAGNETIC HYPNOSIS.*

CONFLAGRATION *INDEED.*

THE ENTIRE *MANSION* IS ABLAZE! *NOTHING* COULD SURVIVE IN THERE!

THE *CLIPPINGS...!*

SIMON?

SIMON, HAVE YOU LOST YOUR *MIND?*

COME *BACK!*

4.19

SIMONNNN!

THE NEXT DAY, I SIFT THROUGH THE **ASHES** OF MIRANDA'S DESTROYED MANSION AND FIND **NOTHING**.

ALL CHARGES AGAINST SIMON HAVE BEEN CLEARED. HIS HEAD-QUARTERS HAS BEEN RELEASED. BUT IT'S HARD TO CELEBRATE THESE EVENTS IN HIS **ABSENCE**.

I'VE GROWN **ACCUSTOMED** TO SIMON OCCASIONALLY VANISHING DURING AN INVESTIGATION.

OFTEN, HE DOES HIS BEST THINKING **ALONE**. THIS, HOWEVER, IS A **NEW** WRINKLE:

DISAPPEARING TO **BEGIN** AN INVESTIGATION... WITHOUT **ME**.

THE BLAST SINGES OUR SKIN, BLINDS US ALL FOR HOURS.

HOURS DURING WHICH I DO NOTHING SAVE LISTEN FOR SIMON'S VOICE...A CLEVER ENTRANCE LINE, A SNIDE REMARK ABOUT THE BARONESS.

IT NEVER SOUNDS.

NO SIGN OF HER, WHICH IS BAD...

...AND NO HINT OF SIMON, WHICH IS GOOD...IF PERPLEXING.

I HEARD HIM. HE WHISPERED SOMETHING ABOUT SOME SORT OF CLIPPINGS. BUT IF THEY WERE IMPORTANT ENOUGH FOR SIMON TO RISK HIS LIFE...

...WHY AREN'T THEY IMPORTANT ENOUGH TO SHARE WITH HIS PARTNER?

4.21

IF HE THINKS THIS IS AN APPROPRIATE TIME FOR HIM TO TAKE A *SOLO WALKABOUT*, HE'S *MISTAKEN*.

THIS TIME, I'M GOING TO *FIND* HIM NO MATTER THAT I HAVE TO PUT ALL OUR *RESOURCES* TO THE *TASK*.

I'M GOING TO FIND HIM AND *CONFRONT* HIM ABOUT THIS.

I'VE GOTTEN THE STRANGE FEELING AS THIS CASE HAS PROGRESSED THAT SIMON DOESN'T *TRUST* ME AS HE USED TO...BUT I CAN'T IMAGINE *WHY*.

WHATEVER THE *REASON* MIGHT BE...

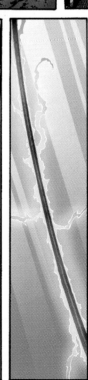

...LET'S HO IT'S NOT *PERMANEN*

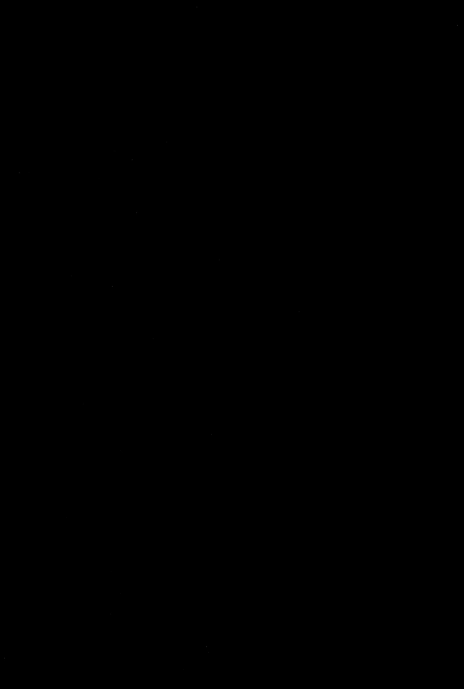

THE PENNY

Afternoon

Copiously Illustrated

OLLYMOP SLAYER
...ANEW

EIGHT DAYS.

THAT'S HOW LONG SIMON'S BEEN **GONE** FOR REASONS **MYSTERIOUS** TO PARTS **UNKNOWN**...

...AND THAT'S HOW LONG I'VE BEEN MAINTAINING THE **PRETENSE** THAT HE'S STILL IN **PARTINGTON**.

AS LOATH AS I AM TO **ADMIT** IT...AFTER ALL, THE MAN'S EGO IS ALREADY THE BIGGEST THING IN THE CITY...THE **ACTIVE PRESENCE OF THE WORLD'S GREATEST DETECTIVE** IS PERHAPS PARTINGTON'S SINGLE GREATEST **CRIME DETERRENT**.

THE **CHARADE** IS **WEARING** ON ME...BUT THE LONG-REBUFFED EMBRACE OF **MORPHEUS** OFFERS NO **REST**. THE MOMENT MY EYES **CLOSE**, MY **WORRIES** TAKE THE FORM OF **NIGHTMARES**. I AM BESET BY VISIONS OF THE **GROTESQUE**...HOT, PANTING BEASTS OF **INDESCRIBABLE HORROR**.

IN MY DELIRIUM, I THINK THEY ARE THE UGLIEST THINGS I HAVE EVER **SEEN**.

I AM **MISTAKEN**.

OP SLAYER

SAY **HI**, CHESTER!

HI! AAAATABOY. HI!

BURF

5.1

5.2

'KAY. ALL THE *AGENTS* WE --

-- I --

-- YOU SENT SPYIN' ON THE CITY'S *BIG CHEESES* -- THEY ALL *AGREE* THAT WHATEVER HOLD THE *BARONESS* HAD ON 'EM IS F'R SURE *GONE*.

THAT *IS* GOOD NEWS.

THOUGH SIMON HAS NO *FULL-TIME EMPLOYEES* PER SE, HE DOES RELY ON CERTAIN *AGENTS* OF ALL WALKS TO SERVE AS HIS *EYES* THROUGHOUT THE CITY.

-- MEANIN' TH' *NASTY* ELEMENT'S ON THE RISE OUT THERE.

SEKOWSKY IS PAID TO GATHER AND *RELAY* THEIR *INFORMATION.* IT'S A MORE APPROPRIATE *JOB* FOR A MAN WHOSE *ODOR* MAKES HIM...LESS *SUBTLE.*

SO I *SEE*...

SOMETHING *ELSE?*

I HEAR *TALK* INNA STREETS, Y'KNOW? RUMOR'S GETTIN' AROUND THAT THE BOSS IS OUTTA *TOWN* --

I DON'T TAKE *ORDERS* FROM NO *SKIRT.*

NO. YOU TAKE THEM FROM THE ASSOCIATE *IN CHARGE* DURING MR. ARCHARD'S *ABSENCE.* IF YOU'RE NOT *UP* TO THAT TASK, I'LL BE *GLAD* TO CABLE SIMON AND ASK FOR THE NAME OF A SUITABLE *REPLACEMENT,* WOULD THAT *SUIT?*

OKAY! OKAY! WE WAS JUST *FUNNIN'!* RIGHT, CHESTER?

BURF

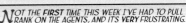

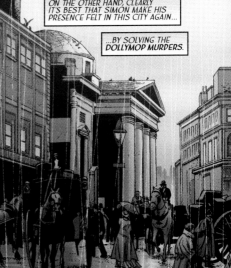

*N*OT THE *FIRST* TIME THIS WEEK I'VE HAD TO PULL RANK ON THE AGENTS, AND ITS *VERY* FRUSTRATING.

ON THE ONE HAND, SIMON'S *VANISHING* GIVES ME THE OPPORTUNITY TO LAY DOWN SOME HIERARCHY AND ASSERT MYSELF.

ON THE OTHER HAND, CLEARLY IT'S BEST THAT SIMON MAKE HIS PRESENCE FELT IN THIS CITY AGAIN...

...BY SOLVING THE *DOLLYMOP MURDERS.*

AS ALWAYS, OUR CONTACTS AT POLICE HEADQUARTERS ARE HAPPY FOR "OUR" HELP. WITHIN MINUTES, I'M INTRODUCED TO THE DETECTIVE HEADING UP THE INVESTIGATION --

--DAVID KINGSLEY-- AT YOUR SERVICE, MISS BISHOP. WE'VE MET BEFORE, YOU KNOW. AT THE POSTLETON GALA.

POSTLETON? WAS I THERE?

THINK BACK. YOU WERE WEARING A CHIFFON DRESS OF A GREEN THAT PERFECTLY MATCHED YOUR EYES.

YOU... ≈KOFF≈ ...YOU REMEMBER THAT?

I'M... OBSERVANT.

PARTICULARLY OF SIGHTS THAT INTRIGUE ME.

OH, MY.

AND TO THINK THIS DAY STARTED BADLY...

QUITE THE FILE. I ADMIRE YOUR DILIGENCE.

THIS CASE HAS ALREADY BECOME FAR TOO PUBLIC. THE DEPARTMENT NEEDS IT QUASHED BEFORE PANIC SPREADS.

SO YOU'RE NOT PUTTING IN THE EXTRA HOURS TO ANGLE FOR PROMOTION?

I VERY MUCH WANT TO BE AN INSPECTOR... SOMEDAY.

I'VE WORKED HARD TOWARDS IT, BUT--MY FIRST PRIORITY IS TO THE PEOPLE OF THIS CITY.

I JUST WANT TO BE A GOOD POLICE-MAN, MISS BISHOP.

GOOD ANSWER.

I LIKE THAT ANSWER.

AMEN. FORGIVE ME FOR PRESUMING, THEN, MR. KINGSLEY--

--BUT SURELY YOU SENSE, AS DO I, THAT HER UNIQUENESS IS THE KEY TO THIS INVESTIGATION.

WITHOUT A DOUBT--BUT I'VE TURNED UP NOTHING SO FAR. HAVE YOU A THEORY?

SIMPLY THAT CASSIE MUST HAVE HAD SOMETHING IN COMMON WITH THE OTHER VICTIMS. THAT'S THE ONLY RATIONAL EXPLANATION AS TO WHY SHE WAS DONE IN.

WITH YOUR PERMISSION, IF I COULD RE-OPEN THAT PART OF THE INVESTIGATION...?

YOU AND SIMON BOTH?

OF...COURSE. MR. ARCHARD IS VERY INVOLVED IN THIS CASE. WE WORK VERY CLOSELY.

HOW... FORTUNATE FOR HIM.

...

...I...

5.4

UR STREETWALKERS D...OR SHOULD I SAY **THREE**?

YOUR DOSSIER TATES THAT **CASSIE** OMMERSBY WAS A RFECTLY RESPECTABLE K **SECRETARY**. MODEST, CE-WORTHY **ATTIRE**... HE DOESN'T FIT THE **PROFILE** AT ALL.

E YOU CERTAIN SAME KILLER IS SPONSIBLE?

UNFORTUNATELY, YES. WHAT WE'VE KEPT FROM THE **PRESS** SO AS TO WEED OUT ANY **FALSE** CONFESSIONS IS THE NATURE OF THE **MURDER WEAPON**.

ALL THE **PUNCTURE WOUNDS** SHOW IT TO BE AN UNUSUAL KNIFE WITH AN ACUTELY CURVED **BLADE**...

...MUCH, IF NOT EXACTLY **LIKE**, **THIS** ONE.

MISS SOMMERSBY WAS SLAIN BY THAT SAME BLADE. I'D STAKE MY REPUTATION ON IT. I **MYSELF** WAS FIRST ON THE SCENE OF HER MURDER AND SAW THE WOUNDS **FRESH**.

FORTUNATELY, MY PRESENCE ALLOWED FOR NO TAMPERING WITH THE CORPSE AFTER THE FACT...NO MISTAKEN IDENTIFICATION OF THE WEAPON.

NO, SHE'S DEFINITELY PART OF THE CHAIN...

...GOD REST HER SOUL.

MUST T TO RK, MR. GSLEY.

"MR. **KINGSLEY**" WAS A THUG WHO RAISED A BOY FOND OF **COPS AND ROBBERS**. CALL ME **DAVID**. I'LL MEET WITH YOU **TOMORROW**, THEN?

ABOUT THE CASE.

MOSTLY.

OH...

...MY.

THE PENNY ARCADIAN
HARTINGTON'S FINEST

EPTING
COACH LINE

SIMON ARCHARD PUT PRO-FESSIONAL FIGHTER PETER GRIMES TO WORK FOLLOWING SIMON'S EXPOSE OF THE PARTINGTON BOXING SYNDICATE.

PETE'S TESTIMONY WAS INVALUABLE, BUT IT COST HIM HIS CAREER--SO SIMON TOOK IT UPON HIMSELF TO MAKE PETE NOT ONLY AN AGENT...

...BUT A GENTLEMAN. UNFORTUNATELY FOR PETE...

⇒HARRUMPH⇐

HOW-DO-YOU-DO-MIS-SUS-SOM-MERS-BY?

...SIMON'S IDEA OF A GENTLEMAN.

POOR PETE. HE FEELS ABOUT AS COMFORTABLE IN A STARCHED COLLAR AS I WOULD DRESSED AS A WHOOPING CRANE.

GOOD EVENING, MR. SOMMERSBY. SAY HELLO, PETER.

HOW-DO-YOU-DO-MIS-TER-SOM-MERS-BY?

STILL, HE PLAYS THE ROLE SIMON SET FOR HIM OUT OF COMPLETE LOYALTY.

I THOUGHT TO BRING PETE ALONG IN CASE I RAN INTO ANY TROUBLE, BUT I AM INSTEAD MET WITH UTTER COURTESY BY CASSIE'S PARENTS...TH FIFTH-GENERATION SOCIAL CENTER O MUCH OF PARTINGTON'S HIGH SOCIET

EVEN USING SIMON'S NAME, THIS WASN'T AN EASY APPOINTMENT TO MAKE. THE SOMMERSBYS, LEGENDARILY PRIVATE TO BEGIN WITH, WERE UNDER-STANDABLY RELUCTANT TO REVISIT THEIR HEARTACHE.

WE CAN'T AFFORD TO RUFFLE ANY FEATHERS HERE UNTIL I LEARN EVERYTHING I--

⇒SNIFF⇐ ⇒SNIFF⇐

MY WORD! DOES ANYONE ELSE--

WHAT IS THAT DREADFUL SMELL?

PFFT. LOOKA THERE. MUSTA STEPPED IN SOME HORSE PIE OUTSIDE.

LEMME JUST GET THAT...

EEEEEK!

-- CAN.

MY BEST LINEN NAPKINS!

I DUNNO 'BOUT BEST ANYMORE. SORRY. DON'T GET YER BUSTL IN A KNOT -- I'LL GET RID OF IT.

I THANK YOU FOR *SEEING* ME. I CANNOT *BEGIN* TO IMAGINE THE PAIN OF YOUR *LOSS* A FEW WEEKS AGO. MR. ARCHARD SENDS HIS *CONDOLENCES* BUT IS *INTENT* ON BRINGING HER KILLER TO *JUSTICE*.

FORGIVE MY *DIRECTNESS*, BUT WHAT CAN YOU TELL ME ABOUT HER *PERSONAL* LIFE? TOO OFTEN, THESE MATTERS CAN BE TRACED TO, SAY, *SPURNED SUITORS*...

NOT *THIS* TIME, I'M AFRAID, MISS BISHOP. CASSIE WAS *BETWEEN* GENTLEMEN CALLERS... *NONE* OF WHOM WAS EVER *WORTH* A *TINKER'S DAMN*, I MIGHT ADD, BUT NONE WE HAVEN'T ALREADY INVESTIGATED *OURSELVES*...

...AND AS FOR HER *GIRLFRIENDS*, THERE AREN'T *ANY* WHO GRIEVE MUCH LESS THAN *WE* DO. NO, OUR CASSIE WAS *VERY* OUTGOING. *QUITE* ACTIVE SOCIALLY.

MR. *GRIMES*, PLEASE FEEL FREE TO MAKE YOURSELF *COMFORTABLE*. WILL YOU *SIT*?

NAW, I'M --

-- I MEAN -- NO *THANK*-YOU-MIS-SUS-*SOM*-MERS-BY.

AND WITH THAT, PETE LOOKS AT ME AND I CAN PRACTICALLY *HEAR* HIM BEGGING MY APPROVAL. I SMILE TO TELL HIM HE'S DOING *FINE*.

NO! IT'S PART OF AN *HEIRLOOM*...

FWOOMPH

...SET...

SVAM
SVAM

I SUPPOSE THE AROMA OF A *FIREPLACE DOES* CARRY THROUGH A *HOUSE* LIKE THAT.

WHO KNEW?

WALK YA BACK T'HEAD-QUARTERS, MIZ EMMA? IT'S NO *TROUBLE*.

I'LL BE FINE, PETE. YOU TAKE CARE.

I...

OKAY.

THE DAWN BRINGS A RELENTLESS PARADE OF AGENTS, EACH BEARING PUZZLE-PIECES OF INFORMATION...

...NONE OF WHICH, SADLY, CONNECT.

I *KNOW* CASSIE'S *EMPLOYERS.* MY HUSBAND AND I MORTGAGE OUR *RESTAURANT* FROM THAT BANK. SURE ENOUGH, EVERYONE THERE SPEAKS *GLOWINGLY* OF HER.

WHEN I SHOWED *PICTURES* OF THE OTHER *VICTIMS,* NOT *ONLY* WAS I *ANGRILY ASSURED* CASSIE WOULD *NEVER* CONSORT WITH SUCH *TROLLOPS...*

...I WAS INFORMED THAT MY BUSINESS WAS NO LONGER *WELCOME* AT THEIR BANK. TELL SIMON HE OWES ME FOR THE COST OF *RE-FINANCING.*

NO *ENEMIES.* SUCH A *BEAUTIFUL* GIRL HAS *NO* JEALOUS BOYFRIENDS IN HER PAST...?

IT'SSSS ENTIRELY *POSSSSSIBLE.* MY CONTACTSSSSS TELL ME THAT SSSSHE WASSSSN'T EXACTLY A...*NICCCCE* GIRL.

SSSEEMS SSSHE WASSS KNOWN AROUND TOWN TO BE RATHER...*EASSSSSY.*

YES. I *DO.* YES. THANK YOU.

YOU GET MY...

THEY SSSAY SSSHE COULD DO THINGSSSS WITH—

DONE. WE'RE *DONE. THANK* YOU, LUCIUS. SSSS.

NUH-UH. GUY'S A *DOCTAH,* I GOTTA TELL YA...

...AN' 'CORDIN' T' THE *PATIENTS* WHAT MATCHED HIS *WORK RECORDS,* THE OL' BOID'S GOT *ALIBIS* TIGHTER'N SIMON'S *WALLET,* 'E DOES. AIN'T *HIM.*

MAYBE IT'S A *MONKEY.* I ONCE SEEN A FELLA TRAIN 'IS *CHIMP* T' RUN DOWN T' THE *CORNER* FOR A *PAPER.*

AND A *CRULLER.* A PAPER *AN'* A CRULLER.

NEVER COUNT OUT DEM *MONKEYS.* DAT'S WHAT *I* SAY.

SO NOTED.

NEXT...?

I THINK I *HAVE* IT. IF YOU TAKE THE HANDS OF THE *CLOCK* AT THE *TIMES OF BIRTH* OF ALL FOUR VICTIMS AND MAP THEM TO THE *SEMAPHORE FLAG CODE,* YOU GET A *KEY WORD.*

WHICH *IS?*

"BURF."

GET OUT.

ALL MORNING LONG, EVERY CRACKPOT SIMON EVER MET SAPS ANOTHER FEW MINUTES OF MY LIFE.

I'M GETTING NOWHERE, AND I'M NOT EVEN MAKING GOOD TIME.

MEMO TO SIMON: EMPLOY FEWER AGENTS WHO RUB THEIR HANDS TOGETHER IN GLEE.

A JEALOUS LOVER, THEN? UNLIKELY. AS LUCK WOULD HAVE IT, ALL THE MEN WE CAN CONNECT WITH CASSIE NO LONGER REMAIN IN PARTINGTON -- RULING THEM OUT AS VENGEFUL SUSPECTS.

THE FACT THAT THEY'VE ALL LEFT TOWN IS LIKELY ATTRIBUTABLE TO CASSIE'S DISAPPROVING PARENTS, WHO -- GIVEN THEIR FINANCIAL STATION -- CAN CERTAINLY "INFLUENCE" THEM TO LEAVE. NO WONDER THE GIRL WASN'T SEEING ANYONE.

WHA' ABOUT HER POP, THEN, LOOV?

MEBBE A LI'L BIT O' TH' OL' CHIM-CHIM, THEN? A LI'L TOO MUCH DADDY'S GIRL, IF YA KNOW?

I CONSIDERED IT, BERT, BUT...

DAVID SENT WORD HE WANTED TO MEET FOR DINNER. THANK GOD.

WHAT'S NEEDED HERE --

-- IS A FRESH PAIR OF EYES.

TWO OF THE VICTIMS WERE IN THE EMPLOY OF THE MADAME LADYBIRD NELL, HERSELF ONE OF OUR MOST RESOURCEFUL AGENTS...

...BUT SHE HAS NO NEW FACTS TO SHARE.

...NO, NONE OF MY GIRLS WERE FAMILIAR WITH MISS SOMMERSBY...

EXCUSE M--

ALDERMAN JONES?

NO.

RIGHT.

NELL, I'M GETTING DESPERATE.

PERHAPS IF I COULD BE WITH YOUR GIRLS...

ABSOLUTELY!

WAIT.

OH, ISN'T SHE JUS' DARLIN'? SHE'LL DO SO WELL!

WE'LL LEAVE YOU TO YOUR WORK, DEAR. YOU'LL REMEMBER EVERYTHING WE TOLD YOU?

NOTHING.

TEN O'CLOCK. ELEVEN. TWELVE. ONE.

FOUR HOURS, AND NOT ONE NIBBLE.

A TERM I USE STRICTLY IN THE **FISHING** SENSE, BY THE WAY. NOT THAT I'M PARTICULARLY **EAGER** TO BE TAKEN SERIOUSLY AS SOME **TOFFER**...

...BUT... I MEAN... IS IT **ME**?

AM I DOING SOMETHING **WRONG**, OR--

OH.

THEN AGAIN, I'M **ONE GIRL** ON **ONE NIGHT.** WHAT ARE THE **ODDS** THAT THE KILLER WILL APPROACH ME JUST BECAUSE I **WANT** HIM TO?

UNSURE OF MYSELF, I WALK **AROUND** A BIT TO MAKE MYSELF A **MOVING TARGET...**

...TRYING TO REMEMBER OVER THE OLFACTORY RACKET OF **LAVENDER TOILET WATER** THE SCENT OF DAVID'S COLOGNE.

DAVID. I CAN'T **REMEMBER** THE LAST TIME A MAN LOOKED AT ME AS HE HAS. LET'S JUST HOPE HE NEVER SEES ME LIKE **THIS.**

THE ONLY THING **WORSE** THAN **THAT** WOULD BE **SIMON** SUDDENLY MATERIALIZING AROUND THE CORNER...

...AN EVENTUALITY EVOKED BY THE FEELING THAT I TRULY **AM** BEING **WATCHED.**

NO **EVIDENCE** OF **SAME,** HOWEVER. NO **FOOTPRINTS,** EVEN. JUST THE TRASH AND DETRITUS OF A **TYPICAL URBAN ALLEYWAY.**

PETE!

PETE, STOP!

PETE, WE **TALKED** ABOUT THIS! WE HAVE TO LET CUSTOMERS APPROACH OR IT'LL LOOK **SUSPICIOUS!**

I KNOW, BUT...WELL...THE WAY THESE GUYS **LOOK** AT YA...IT'S...THEY'RE...

...I JUST CAN'T **HELP** IT, MISS EMMA.

SIGH.

AND HE HONESTLY **CAN'T.** WHEN WE SAY SOMEONE'S LOYAL TO A **FAULT,** THIS IS **PRECISELY** WHAT WE MEAN. NO, IF WE'RE TO STAND **ANY** CHANCE OF SNARING OUR PREDATOR...

...WE'LL NEED A **NEW** APPROACH.

MOMMY...?

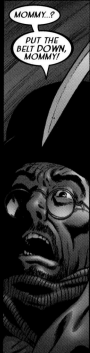

MOMMY...?

PUT THE BELT DOWN, MOMMY!

SOMEBODY SAY "BELT"?

FWAM

OLD STORY. DOMESTIC VIOLENCE AS A BOY, etc., etc. HERE'S HIS *FILE*. JOB HISTORY, ARREST AND MEDICAL REPORTS....

...IF YOU CAN CONSTRUCT A *PSYCHOLOGICAL PROFILE* FOR THE LIKES OF *HIM*, WE'LL START MEASURING *YOU* FOR A JACKET.

IT WOULDN'T TAKE *MUCH*.

DESPITE THE INSPECTOR'S *SNIDE CRACK*, WHITSON IS *TEXTBOOK*. EVERYTHING HERE *POINTS* TO SOMEONE WHO'D...

...

OH MY GOD.

IN THE NEXT HALF-HOUR, MY THOUGHTS ARE LED DOWN AN ENTIRELY *NEW*... AND VERY *DARK*...AVENUE. WHERE IS...

HE *CONFESSED?* *IMMEDIATELY?*

YOU'D THINK AFTER ALL *THAT*, HE COULD PUT UP A *LITTLE* FIGHT. THIS IS THE MOST ANTICLIMACTIC CASE I'VE EVER *SEEN*.

WELL, I'M *SORRY* THIS ADVENTURE ISN'T UP TO MR. ARCHARD'S ORDINARILY *SCINTILLATING STANDARDS*, MISS BISHOP, BUT NOT *EVERY* MURDERER IS A *BRILLIANT MASTERMIND*.

IN FACT, *DESPITE* THE FACT THAT IN HIS DEMENTIA HE'S TAKING CREDIT FOR CRIMES COMMITTED BEFORE HE WAS EVEN *BORN*, MR. *DANIEL WHITSON* IS ANYTHING *BUT* A CRIMINAL GENIUS.

I *KNOW* THIS BECAUSE WE'VE LOCKED HIM UP OVERNIGHT MORE THAN *ONCE* ON DRUNK AND *DISORDERLY* CHARGES.

UNTIL *TONIGHT*, HOWEVER, WE ASSUMED HIS PSYCHOTIC RAVINGS CAME FROM A *BOTTLE*.

POLICE

DETECTIVE KINGSLEY! WHERE *IS* HE? I HAVE TO *SPEAK* TO HIM *IMMEDIATELY!*

NOT HIS *SHIFT*, EM.

TRY CALLING HIS *HOUSE*.

OPERATOR'LL PUT YOU RIGHT *THROUGH* IF HE'S THERE.

SURE ENOUGH, HE ANSWERS ON THE THIRD RING.

HELLO, *DAVID?*

THANK GOD I *FOUND* YOU, DAVID. I NEED YOU TO MEET ME AT THE ARCHARD *HEADQUARTERS*. YES, *RIGHT AWAY*.

NO. WAIT. GIVE ME AN *HOUR*. BUT, DAVID... I'VE FOUND SOMETHING THAT SHEDS A WHOLE NEW *LIGHT* ON CASSIE'S *MURDER*.

DAVID, I'VE BROKEN THE *CASE*.

FINE. I'LL SEE YOU *THERE...*

...RIGHT AFTER I HAVE ANOTHER CHAT WITH THE SOMMERSBYS.

5.17

EMMA, IS EVERYTHING ALL RIGHT? YOU MADE IT SOUND SO *URGENT.*

WHAT DID YOU *FIND?*

THAT I'VE BEEN WRONG ALL *ALONG* ABOUT CASSIE. THERE *WAS* NO COMMON ELEMENT LINKING HER TO THE OTHERS, DAVID...

...BECAUSE *WHITSON* DIDN'T *KILL HER.*

WHAT? DID HE *SAY* THAT?

HE DIDN'T *HAVE* TO. I *READ* IT. IN A *POLICE REPORT.*

THE NIGHT CASSIE WAS *KILLED,* DAVID... WHITSON WAS IN THE *DRUNK TANK.*

DANIEL WHITSON WAS A *MADMAN* WHO KILLED *RANDOM PROSTITUTES.* SOME- ONE CLEVERLY *SANE* TARGETED OUR *CASSIE.*

ONE WHO... GOOD *LORD!*...TOOK INSPIRATION FROM THE *DOLLYMOP KILLINGS* AND TRIED TO FOLD CASSIE *INTO* THEM AS A *COVER-UP!*

EMMA, WE HAVE TO TELL THE DEPARTMENT *IMMEDIATELY!* THIS MEANS THERE'S A *COPYCAT KILLER* STILL ON THE *LOOSE!*

BUT NOT *EVERY* MAN CAN BE BULLIED INTO LEAVING *BEHIND* EVERYTHING HE *KNOWS,* NOT EVEN BY A *SOMMERSBY.* SOME HAVE *CAREERS*--LOCAL *TIES.* I'D GUESS WE'RE LOOKING FOR THE ONE WHO HAD STRONG REASONS TO *STAY.*

THE ONE WHO, TOO LATE, SAW WHAT WAS *COMING*--AND *KILLED* CASSIE *BEFORE* SHE COULD REVEAL HIM AND DESTROY HIS *LIFE.*

BUT THAT'S JUST *IT.*

HE'S *NOT.*

5.18

ALL RIGHT. ALL RIGHT. THEN WE START FROM *SCRATCH*. WHO HAS *MOTIVE?* A *CO-WORKER?* AN ANGRY *PARENT?* LET'S GO SPEAK WITH HER *FAMILY* AGAIN.

ALREADY *DONE*.

I REMEMBERED HOW *DISMISSIVE* THEY WERE OF HER *EX-BOYFRIENDS* AND ASKED MYSELF: SUPPOSE THERE WERE MORE *TO* THAT? OUR *SECOND* CONVERSATION FORCED MUCH OF *THIS* OUT IN THE OPEN:

CASSIE WASN'T SIMPLY *PROMISCUOUS*, DAVID.

SHE WAS, IN FACT, A *NYMPHOMANIAC*. A *SEX ADDICT*. AND A RATHER *RAUNCHY* ONE, AT *THAT*-- SOMETHING HER UPPER-CRUST PARENTS WORKED *HARD* TO KEEP *SECRET*.

YOU'RE *JOKING*.

NO. THE PATTERN WAS ALWAYS THE *SAME*: CASSIE, RESENTFUL OF HER PARENTS' *CONTROLLING NATURE*, WOULD DRAW A LOVER INTO A *SECRET AFFAIR* UNTIL HE *BORED* HER--

--THEN *END* THE RELATIONSHIP AND CONFESS THE DIRTY DETAILS TO HER *FATHER* JUST TO *SPITE* HIM.

I DON'T THINK SOMMERSBY FORCED HER EX-LOVERS OUT OF *PARTINGTON* BECAUSE HE *DISAPPROVED* OF THEM. HE DID IT SO THEY COULDN'T *SPREAD* CASSIE'S DISGRACEFUL SECRET. HIS ENTIRE *SOCIAL STATION* HINGED ON THEIR *SILENCE*.

HE'S BEEN *CAUGHT*.

IT *HAD* TO BE ONE OF THE FEW OFFICERS WHO KNEW ABOUT THE *SPECIAL BLADE* WHITSON USED...BUT *ALL* OF THEM HAVE *ALIBIS* FOR THAT NIGHT. IF YOU'LL *RECALL*, YOU *YOURSELF* TOLD ME WHERE *YOU* WERE.

THEN *END* THE RELATIONSHIP AND CONFESS THE DIRTY DETAILS TO HER *FATHER* JUST TO *SPITE* HIM.

YOU WERE *THE FIRST ON THE SCENE OF THE MURDER.*

DAVID...

...YOU'RE THE *KILLER*.

6.4

AS USUAL, SIMON MOVES CONTRARY TO *PUBLIC OPINION*...

...BUT IT MEANS WE'RE UPON THE *CRIME SCENE* BEFORE THE *SCREAMING* DIES DOWN, AND BEFORE THE CROWD CAN EVEN *ARTICULATE* THE NOTION OF HAVING WITNESSED A *MURDER*...

...SIMON'S GATHERING *CLUES.*

EMMA, GET ME THE VICTIM'S *TOPCOAT!*

BUT THE *MURDERER* --

GET THE *COAT!*

UNNNNHHHH...

-- THE *MURDERER* IS STILL ON THE *LOOSE*, SIMON!

THE *MAGICIAN!* DID YOU *SEE* HIM?

THUNDERED RIGHT...*PAST ME*, HE DID. ELBOWED ME AWFUL *HARD*... IN M'*NOGGIN*...!

GONE. YOU'RE THE *STAGE MANAGER?*

HOW DID YOU--?

THE COLLECTION OF *KEYS*. YOU SAW YOUR ASSAILANT *CLEARLY?*

YES, SIR. IT WAS *DEFINITELY*--

THE CONTUSION BEHIND HIS *EAR* INDICATES THE MAN WAS BLUDGEONED *UNCONSCIOUS* BEFORE BEING *DROWNED*, BUT HE'S BEEN *STRIPPED* OF ANY FURTHER *IDENTIFICATION*. WHAT'S IN HIS *COAT?*

NOT *MUCH*. A *HOTEL KEY*, A POUCH OF *TOBACCO*, AND SOME *CIGARETTE PAPERS*.

CIGARETTES...

--CORRADINO? YOU MEAN HE DROWNED AN *INNOCENT STRANGER* CHOSEN AT *RANDOM?*

IMAGINE. ONLY *TEN WORDS* IN THAT SENTENCE, AND YET *THREE* OF THEM ARE *WRONG.*

THE *VICTIM*-- HARDLY *"INNOCENT"*-- IS A DETECTIVE WITH THE *BEETON AGENCY.* IT ISN'T COMMON *KNOWLEDGE,* BUT THEY WEAR SPECIAL *SIGNET RINGS* SO AS TO QUIETLY *IDENTIFY* THEMSELVES TO ONE ANOTHER.

WORKING THIS FAR OUT OF *TOWN,* HE MUST HAVE BEEN *TRAILING* SOMEONE --LIKELY CORRADINO *HIMSELF,* JUDGING BY THE *CIRCUMSTANCES*-- WHICH MEANS HE WAS *HARDLY* CHOSEN AT *"RANDOM."* KILLING HIM PUT AN *END* TO HIS *INVESTIGATION.*

SIMON?

SIMON!

HMM? OH. YES.

EMMA, PHONE THAT HOTEL *IMMEDIATELY.*

AND...?

AND ASK IF WE'VE TIME TO STOP CORRADINO'S *SECOND* MURDER.

6.7

...BROUGHT HIM TO THE *HOSPITAL* SOON AS WE *COULD,* MR. ARCHARD.

HE'LL BE *UNCONSCIOUS* FOR A WHILE, BUT HE'LL *LIVE.*

WE FOUND HIM IN HIS ROOM. THE *POISON* CAME IN A MEAL DELIVERED BY *KITCHEN SERVICE.* HAD YO NOT WARNED US IN *TIME,* HE'D MOST CERTAINLY BE *DEAD* BY NOW.

THANK YOU, DOCTOR. WE'LL *CALL* FOR YOU IF HE *AWAKENS.*

BY DELIBERATELY SPLITTING THEM *UP.*

CORRADINO -- A GUEST AT THE *SAME HOTEL* -- GIFTED ALL THE ROOMS WITH *V.I.P. TICKETS* --

-- BUT THROUGH AN *"OVERSIGHT,"* THESE GENTLEMEN RECEIVED *ONE,* NOT *TWO.*

ACCORDING TO THESE *PAPERS* -- WHICH CORRADINO *ALSO* WOULD HAVE STOLEN HAD WE GIVEN HIM *TIME* -- A STRING OF HIGH-PROFILE *ROBBERIE* COINCIDES WITH HIS *TRAVELS.* THAT'S WHY THE *BEETON MEN* WERE *TRAILING* HIM -- AND HE *KNEW* THAT.

BUT IF CORRADINO WERE *EVADIN* THE LAW...

SIMON, HOW DID YOU KNOW...? THE *FIRST* VICTIM'S FINGERS SHOWED NO *NICOTINE* STAINS... YET HE'D PURCHASED TOBACCO AND CIGARETTE PAPERS FOR *SOMEONE*, PRESUMABLY A *TRAVELING COMPANION*...AND THE *BEETON* OPERATIVES TRAVEL IN *PAIRS*.

GIVEN THAT FAR MORE *MEN* THAN *WOMEN* ENGAGE IN THE NASTY HABIT OF ROLLING *CIGARETTES*, ODDS WERE THAT COMPANION WAS HIS *INVESTIGATIVE PARTNER* -- AND THUS ANOTHER *TARGET*.

SINCE CORRADINO COULDN'T COMMIT *BOTH* MURDERS ON *STAGE*, HE ARRANGED FOR THE *POISON*...NO DOUBT ONE OF *MANY* CONTINGENCIES...

...THEN STOLE THE FIRST VICTIM'S *IDENTIFICATION* HOPING TO *STALL* ME...

...GIVING THIS MAN TIME TO *DIE*.

William Corradine
a.k.a. **"The Astounding Corradino"**

...ink suspected between suspect's **touring dates** and mysterious robberies committed **dates** same. Keep Cor...

...llar...

BUT HOW COULD CORRADINO *POSSIBLY* SURMISE ONLY *ONE* OF THEM WOULD COME TO HIS *SHOW*?

SIMON, WE *ALSO* RECEIVED V.I.P. TICKETS. WHAT *CONCEIVABLE* REASON WOULD CORRADINO HAVE TO INVITE THE WORLD'S *FOREMOST* DETECTIVE TO THE *SCENE* OF HIS *CRIME*?

TO *TAUNT* ME. ALL OF THIS *CONFIRMS* WHAT I'D ALREADY *SUSPECTED*... I AND, APPARENTLY, *MIRANDA CROSS*, WHO GATHERED *NEWSPAPER CLIPPINGS* ON OUR MAGICIAN.

"CORRADINO" IS BUT AN *ALIAS* THE MAN MAINTAINS.

HIS TRUE NAME IS *LIGHTBOURNE*.

6.9

ENTER, STAGE LEFT.

THE NIGHT IS *FULL* OF SURPRISES.

MEANING?

WELL, I SEE YOU DON'T WEAR *ANGER* VERY COMFORTABLY.

NOR *YOU* THE ROLE OF *PSYCHOANALYST.* THE *DEDUCTIVE MIND* HAS NO *USE* FOR *ANGER.* THERE-FORE, I AM *NOT ANGRY.*

YOU'RE *SOMETHING.*

YOU WER *CORREC* ABOUT TH *STAGING*

SIMON, I'M *SERIOUS.* UP UNTIL YOU MENTIONED HIS *NAME,* I'D BELIEVED HIM *DEAD.*

AS HAD *I.*

AND YET YOU'RE ABSOLUTELY *SURE* IT'S *HIM?*

ALMOST. YES, LIKE *CORRADINO,* LIGHTBOURNE WAS A *DEVOTEE* OF *STAGE MAGIC...*BUILDING *TRAPS* AND *GADGETS* WAS HIS *HOBBY...* BUT THAT HARDLY MAKES FOR *CONCLUSIVE IDENTIFICATION.* NO...

...THERE'S ONL' ONE WAY TO G *IRREFUTABLE* PROOF...

NO DOUBT THE FIRST MAN RECEIVED A WHISPERED *WARNING* TO PLAY *ALONG* AND STAY *PUT* UNTIL AFTER THE *SHOW...*

...THEN WAS SECRETLY LOWERED THROUGH WHAT'S KNOWN AS A *CAULDRON TRAP.*

I'D *FORGOTTEN.* YOU HAVE SOME THEATER BACKGROUND.

DO YOU MISS *PERFORMING?*

WHY? ARE YOU TRYING TO GET *RID* OF ME?

I'M NOT THE *MAGICIAN* HERE.

I SUPPOSE I MISS VENUES LIKE *THIS.* SUPERB *ACOUSTICS,* GAS *FOOTLIGHTS.* SOMETIMES...

...SOMETIMES YOU AND I *BOTH* ALLOW THE PAST TO *ENCROACH* A BIT.

SIMON, *PLEASE* TELL ME MORE ABOUT THIS *"LIGHTBOURNE"* CHARACTER.

HE WAS YOUR FORMER *PARTNER. THAT,* I *KNOW...*BUT NOT MUCH *MORE.* YOU *NEVER* SPEAK OF HIM.

THEN YOU'RE *USED* TO IT. GOOD.

...AND THAT'S TO *DUPLICATE* HIS *FINALE.*

SIMON, HAVE YOU LOST YOUR --

HELP ME OR *GO AWAY.* I'M NOT INTERESTED IN *BANTERING.*

...

FINE. BUT TELL ME HOW THIS *HELPS* YOU.

LIGHTBOURNE INVENTED AND SHARED WITH ME CERTAIN *ESCAPE MECHANISMS...* FALSE HINGES, TRICK LOCKS AND THE LIKE.

IF I *RECOGNIZE* THEM AS STEPS IN THE *ESCAPE* PROCEDURE, THEY'RE PRACTICALLY THE *SIGNATURE* TO HIS *CONFESSION.*

AND THE *BLINDFOLD?* DOES IT SECRETLY CONTAIN ANYTHING THAT WOULD *HELP?*

NO.

THEN *THERE,* I DRAW THE *LINE.*

ONE OF US HAS TO BE SANE.

6.11

'E'S PROBABLY *RIGHT.* I'VE LITTLE DOUBT HE CAN DO THIS. THAT'S NOT WHAT'S WORRYING ME.

MY *CONCERN* IS THAT SIMON IS ACTING WITH *UNCHARACTERISTIC EMOTION* --

YOU THERE -- GET *AWAY* FROM THAT!

THERE'S BEEN A MAN *MURDERED* HERE AND --

-- *OH!* IT'S *YOU!* BEGGING Y'R *PARDON,* MIZ BISHOP. SO, C'N YER BOSS *EXPLAIN* ANY O'THESE *GOINGS-ON* TO A LOWLY *STAGE MANAGER...?*

WOULD *THAT,* KIND SIR. MR. ARCHARD HAS HIS *LEADS,* BUT HE'S CHOSEN A RATHER *UNCHARACTERISTIC* MANNER IN WHICH TO *PURSUE* THEM.

WHATEVER'S RATTLIN' THROUGH 'IS SKULL, IT'S BEYOND YOU 'N' *I, THAT'S* F'RSURE. IT'S *HIS SHOW.*

REGULAR FOLKS LIKE *US,* ALL WE C'N DO IS JUST STAND HERE *STAGE RIGHT* 'N' WATCH 'IM *WORK.*

THAT *IS* SOMETIMES THE *CASE* -- THOUGH I CONFESS I'M BEGINNING TO FEEL IT HAPPENING *MORE* AND M --

6.13

THIS IS STAGE *LEFT*.

LIGHTBOURNE.

SPEAKING.

AND THE *REAL* STAGE MANAGER?

IT'S OVER *HERE*.

HIM? LAST I SAW OF *HIM*, HE WAS *OVERWROUGHT* ABOUT THE *MURDER*.

THE POOR MAN SIMPLY WENT TO *PIECES*.

"NOW...I SEE SIMON'S FOUND THE *LOCKPICK* SECRETED ON THE UNDER-SIDE OF A CHAIN LINK."

EXCELLENT.

"HE KNOWS THE *SEAMS* ON THE *STRAITJACKET*, IRON-STRONG DURING ANY *EXAMINATION*, *DISSOLVE* IN WATER.

"THAT *ALONE* IS *QUITE* THE LIFESAVER, BY THE WAY. I'M QUITE *PROUD* OF THAT ONE.

"BRAVO, SIMON!"

"NOW THE *FINAL* GIMMICK. SIMON RECALLS THIS ONE, *TOO*. THE *LID* CONTAINS A HIDDEN DOOR THAT CAN PROVIDE *EGRESS*...

"...WHEN IT'S NOT WELDED *SHUT*."

"LOOK AT HIM GO. DOES HE REMEMBER..?

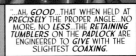

"...AH, *GOOD*...THAT WHEN HELD AT *PRECISELY* THE PROPER ANGLE...NO MORE, NO *LESS*...THE *RETAINING TUMBLERS* ON THE *PADLOCK* ARE ENGINEERED TO *GIVE* WITH THE SLIGHTEST *COAXING*.

YOU -- YOU'RE *INSANE!*

NO, BUT I *AM* PETTY.

TH-THEY'LL CATCH YOU! *SOMEONE* WILL --

PROBABLY. IF I'M WEARING *BLOOD-SPATTERED CLOTHES*. SO *THAT* WON'T DO.

STILL...I'M *IMAGINATIVE.*

...GAS FLAME!

FWOOSH

AAH!

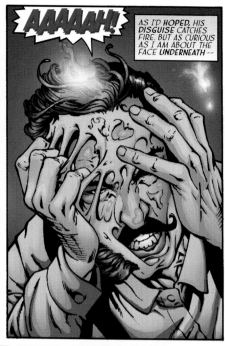

AAAAAH!

AS I'D HOPED, HIS DISGUISE CATCHES FIRE. BUT AS CURIOUS AS I AM ABOUT THE FACE UNDERNEATH--

AND THUS I HEAR THE SOUND OF LIGHTBOURNE'S FLEEING FOOTSTEPS--

→KOFF!
KOFF!←

--UNDER THE NOISE OF GEYSERING WATER.

SIMON, ARE YOU ALL RIGHT? HURRY UP AND GET YOUR BREATH BACK SO YOU CAN COUGH OUT A WORD OR TWO OF GRATITUDE.

YOU BROKE →KOFF← BROKE THE GLASS...

Oh, PLEASE! YOU'LL SPOIL ME WITH THAT KIND OF TALK AND--

OH

—LET HIM *BURN.*

I HAVE *OTHER* PRIORITIES.

KSSSH

HOW DARE YOU?

I HAD IT *UNDER CONTROL!* I DIDN'T REQUIRE YOUR *ASSISTANCE!* I COULD HAVE *ESCAPED!* I COULD HAVE—

SIMON, I—I'M *SORRY!* I HAD NO *INTENTION* OF *UNDERMINING* YOU! I MERELY BELIEVED YOU WERE IN *DANGER!*

SIMON, PLEASE *SAY* SOMETHING.

SETTLE *DOWN,* EMMA.

YOU'VE DONE NOTHING TO *APOLOGIZE* FOR.

NOW... WHAT PRECISELY HAVE YOU BEEN *UP* TO THESE LAST SIX MINUTES...?

6.21

...AND WHILE I *FREED* YOU, LIGHTBOURNE *ESCAPED*.

SIMON, THOSE *CLIPPINGS* YOU WERE SO DESPERATE TO SALVAGE FROM MIRANDA CROSS' MANSION... DID THEY HAVE ANYTHING TO DO WITH...

...MY EX-PARTNER? PERHAPS. WE CAN DISCUSS THAT LATER. YOU SAY YOU LIBERATED A *BANDANA*...?

YOU MEAN *THIS?* I SUPPOSE I GRABBED IT *FROM* HIM WITHOUT TRULY *THINKING* ABOUT IT. IS IT *SIGNIFICANT?*

YES.

AND YOU'LL TELL ME WHY WHEN YOU *FEEL* LIKE IT?

YES.

WELL, SPLENDID. THAT'S THE SIMON I *KNOW*...

...*NOT* THE SIMON WHO SO UNCHARACTERISTICALLY *EXPLODED* MOMENTS AGO. I'VE *NEVER* SEEN HIM LIKE THAT. EVER.

WHAT IS IT ABOUT THIS OLD ALLY OF SIMON'S THAT CAN BRING *OUT* SUCH BEHAVIOR?

WHAT *IS* THE MYSTERY OF LIGHTBOURNE?